Steven Camden is one of the UK's most acclaimed spoken-word artists. He also writes plays and teaches storytelling. In 2013 he set up Bearheart, his own story-based creative projects company. Steven lives in London, but Birmingham is where he's from. TAPE is Steven's first novel. When you have read it you will find this hard to believe.

Follow Steven on Twitter
@homeofpolar

www.facebook.com/stevencamdentheauthor

Also by Steven Camden

IT'S ABOUT LOVE

Praise for TAPE

TAPE was nominated for the Carnegie Medal and shortlisted for the Leeds Book Award.

'Gripping...cleverly structured and movingly characterised.' *The Sunday Times*

'Deftly structured...an impressive debut.' *Telegraph*

'Beautifully controlled – a tender love story about grief, regret, healing and hope...builds to a wonderfully rewarding ending.' *Daily Mail*

'Steven Camden is a born storyteller. Read TAPE, rewind, then read it again.' Phil Earle

'Original, playful...full of heart.' Laura Dockrill

TAPE

STEVEN CAMDEN

HarperCollins *Children's Books*

First published in hardback in Great Britain by HarperCollins *Children's Books* in 2014
This edition published in Great Britain by HarperCollins *Children's Books* in 2015
HarperCollins *Children's Books* is a division of HarperCollins*Publishers* Ltd,
1 London Bridge Street, London, SE1 9GF

The HarperCollins website address is: www.harpercollins.co.uk

1

Printed and bound in England by Clays Ltd, St Ives plc

For Yael

Half of me is you

X

8

Hello? Is it on? Yeah, I can see the light. It's on. I'm starting again. I'm recording.

That just happened. That actually just happened and the crazy thing is it didn't even feel weird. I think I get it now, Dad. I think I understand.

It's probably best not to think about it too much, right?

The universe and everything.

I'm here. That's what matters. I'm here doing this and it happened. Just like you said, so I guess the universe is happy.

Was it always meant to be now? Sorry, I'll leave it alone.

Everything happens when it should.

This is what you did, sitting down and pressing record, and now it's gonna be what I do.

I'm talking into the speaker — how does that even work?

Everybody always said, 'It's important to get stuff out, Ameliah, put it down, it's part of moving on.' I never really listened.

I guess I just didn't want to do it their way. Maybe I wasn't ready, I dunno.

This feels different. This feels right.

So much has happened. There's so much to say, so I'm gonna say it.

It's half twelve now and I'm recording my voice on to this tape.

Just like you.

CHAPTER 1

Ryan wiped the condensation from the small circular bathroom mirror with his fingers and imagined he was scraping ice from the window of a dug-up frozen submarine. A World War II sub discovered near the North Pole years after it was lost at sea. He pictured seeing the solid face of some old naval officer, frost in his moustache, eyes wide, staring out, frozen in the panic of realising he was about to be stuck forever.

He lowered his hand and saw only his own face, thirteen years old, flushed from the heat of the bath, his thick dark hair slicked back from getting out of the water.

Whenever Ryan looked into the mirror he felt an urge to slap himself in the face. Not because he was angry with himself and thought he deserved it, more because he'd seen it in a film once. The private investigator character staring at himself in the mirror after a crazy night of action and danger and slapping himself to make sure he was focused for a new day on the job.

Ryan lifted his hand level with the side of his face. He tensed the muscles in his arm, pulling his hand back ready to strike. His eyes narrowed as he prepared for the slap. Then he froze, staring at himself.

— Come on, you chicken, do it. Do it!

He let out a sigh, puffing out his cheeks as his arm moved back down to his side, and thought about how much space there was inside his mouth. How you could probably fit half a good-sized orange in each side between the teeth and your cheek.

— Yo!

The voice from outside the door came with a bang that shook the hinges and popped the air out of Ryan's face.

— I said yo! You better hurry up, weed, or I'll fold you in half.

Ryan stared at himself as the banging carried on.

He pictured Nathan's face on the other side of the door, getting more and more angry, twisting into shapes like some kind of mutant monster stepbrother. He reached for another towel and threw it over his head and shoulders like a boxer, getting himself ready for the title fight.

It was just over six months since Dad sat him down and told him that Sophia would be moving in and bringing Nathan too. Dad had asked him what he thought and he'd said it was a good idea because he'd seen the hope in Dad's eyes. They moved in the next week, which made Ryan realise it really didn't matter what he thought.

At least he didn't have to share his room. Dad's gesture to turn his office into a bedroom for Nathan meant Ryan at least got to keep his own space, although Nathan didn't seem all that clued up about the rules of privacy. He never knocked. He just barged in like he owned the place.

He was four months younger and yet a couple of inches taller and, truth be told, a lot stronger, although Ryan put that down to the fact that he seemed to eat non-stop. He even slept with a sandwich next to his pillow.

A month later Dad and Sophia got married in a small grey room in the council building. Ryan wore the same suit he'd worn to his mum's funeral. Back then it had been baggy; this time it fitted like a glove.

The night of the wedding Sophia had cornered him in the kitchen, when Ryan was trying to find more cherryade, and told him that she wasn't trying to replace his mum. That she loved his dad very much and wanted this to be a new start for everyone. Ryan had seen the look on her round face as she stood there awkwardly in too much make-up, her dark hair tied up, wearing her peach dress with frilly edges. Ryan had smiled and said that's what he wanted as well and Sophia had hugged him slightly too tight and the pop bottle had fallen out of his hand.

When she went back to the living room, Ryan picked up the bottle and watched the bubbles inside fight to get to the top. Nathan came into the kitchen to get more food. He told Ryan his suit looked stupid. Ryan said nothing. Nathan saw the bottle of pop and snatched it. Ryan went to say something then stopped himself, stepped back and watched Nathan twist the bottle lid and soak himself in cherryade.

Ryan pulled on his Chicago Bears sleeping T-shirt and stared at his boom box. The shiny silver panels caught the light. The clean black buttons underneath the little windows that let you see the tape inside. The super bass circular speakers. Perfect. It had been his gift the Christmas before Mum died. He remembered tearing open the paper and seeing the corner of the box, spending the rest of the day in his pyjamas tuning the radio dial to all the different stations he could find.

Ryan pulled open the narrow drawer of his bedside table and took out a cassette box. Its white sleeve was empty of any writing. He ran his thumb along the edge of the box, feeling the plastic edge, then eased the box open and took out the tape.

He looked at the thin white label as he slotted the tape into cassette deck two. In block capital dark blue felt tip, the word MUM.

Ryan pressed rewind and wiped the little window with his fingertip as the tape motor hummed, spooling the tape back to the beginning.

The rewind button clicked up. Ryan moved the boom box to the edge of his bedside table so he could speak into it while lying in bed and, with two fingers, pressed the play and record buttons at the same time. The little red indicator light blinked on as the tape spooled round showing it was recording. Ryan cleared his throat.

Ameliah stares at what's left of her cornflakes. Her spoon makes waves in her bowl as her slender fingers turn it and she imagines each soggy flake is a tiny wooden raft floating in a milky white sea.

She moves her spoon in between them and watches as some sink, while others fight to stay afloat. Morning light cuts across the kitchen floor through the big window.

— Penny for 'em, Nan says from across the small square table through a mouthful of crumpet.

Ameliah knows what that means, she's heard it plenty of times before (mostly from Nan), but only this time does it occur to her that one penny for what someone is thinking seems like a really cheap deal.

— I've never been in a boat.

Nan stops chewing for a second to listen then carries on. Ameliah looks at her.

— I mean in proper water, like the sea.

Nan starts to spread butter on to another crumpet from the pile on the plate between them.

— You're still young, love. There's plenty of time.

She smiles as she pushes the new crumpet into her mouth.

— How old were you? asks Ameliah. When you went on your first boat?

— Me? Oh, now you're asking. It was probably with your granddad, long before you were born. Before I had your mum.

Ameliah looks down. A strand of dark curls falls across her face. She sweeps it back behind her ear with her fingertips.

— Are you sure you don't want a crumpet, love, strength for your last day?

Ameliah shakes her head.

— No thanks, Nan.

Nan takes another crumpet from the pile.

— She wasn't a breakfast person either.

Ameliah looks at Nan and tries to imagine her younger, sitting across a table from Mum, a pile of crumpets between them, Mum daydreaming about school.

— I guess it's genes, continues Nan, although she certainly didn't get it from me.

Ameliah shrugs. Nan leans forward.

— Are you keeping up with your journal, like the lady said?

Ameliah pictures the empty journal pushed under her bed, the light brown recycled cover, the pages clean and new. She looks into her bowl. All but one of the tiny rafts have sunk. She stares at it, clinging on to the surface.

— Kind of. It feels weird.

— It will do, love, for a while, but trust me, it's—

— Important to get stuff out.

Nan smiles and lets out an old-lady laugh through a mouthful of crumpet.

— That's my girl.

Ameliah stares at the last flake clinging on to the surface of her milk as it bobs alone, refusing to sink.

Ryan stared out of the classroom window across the school playing fields. The grey sky heavy with rain ready to fall. He saw a group of girls jogging in a loose pack, doing laps of the pitch, too far away to see faces. He focused on one girl, near the back, her dark hair bouncing against her shoulders as she moved.

— Ryan!

Miss Zaidel was standing in front of his desk. Everyone else in the class was watching.

— Do you have any thoughts?

Her voice was angry. Ryan looked across the room and saw Nathan smiling his smug smile.

— Sorry, Miss, I was—

— You were miles away, Ryan. Again. That's what.

— Yes, Miss.

— It's been like this all term, Ryan.

— Yes, Miss. Sorry, Miss.

Nathan pulled a face from across the room. Ryan scowled back at him.

— Right, well, if you've finished watching the girls outside, would you mind coming back and joining us for our last lesson together?

People giggled. Nathan's smug stepbrother smile widened. Ryan felt his cheeks getting hot.

— Yes, Miss.

Miss Zaidel returned to the front of the class.

— Right, so can anyone else answer my question? How long has John Major been Prime Minister?

Nathan's hand shot up into the air.

— I can, Miss. Three years, Miss.

Miss Zaidel nodded.

— Thank you, Nathan, and somebody else? Who did he take over from?

Nathan smiled straight at Ryan as the rest of the class stuck up their hands. Ryan ground his teeth as the sky rolled thunder outside and it started to rain.

Ameliah scans the lunchtime selection in front of her. The dinner lady stares at her. Ameliah doesn't recognise the lady, but she knows that stare. She's felt it enough times. It's the stare people give when they know about her parents and feel they should say something, but don't really have a clue what words to use.

She grabs a ham roll and a carton of juice and moves away before the dinner lady can speak. As she queues up to pay, she thinks about how six months have flown by. She thinks about Dad, how he changed in the months after Mum. How the illness made him shrink.

— Is that everything, sweetheart?

Ameliah snaps out of her daydream. Corine on the cafeteria till smiles her Cheshire cat smile like always. The gap between her top front teeth big enough to fit a five-pence piece.

— No crisps today?

Ameliah smiles back.

— Not today thanks, Corine.

Across the room she spots Heather, sitting with some of the others, flapping her arms like a bird, calling her over. Ameliah sighs.

— Chin up, love.

Corine's face is round and warm like the grandmas in fairy tales and, as she makes her way through the busy lunch hall towards the table of girls, Ameliah decides that Corine would get on really well with Nan.

In the noisy lunch hall Ryan sat staring into space with a mouthful of ham roll. The seat opposite him was empty. He shook his head as he thought about being embarrassed in class earlier.

Liam sat down like a horse crashing into a fence.

— Summertime!

Ryan jumped.

— Got you! Big L strikes again.

— I told you not to do that!

Liam smiled and dropped his Tupperware lunch box on to the table.

— I know, but it's too easy, man.

He rubs his shovel hands together.

— Half a day left, Ryan, then six sweet weeks of freedom.

— Sit down, will ya? People are staring.

— What you got?

— I dunno.

— You're eating it.

— Oh, ham.

— You got crisps?

— Monster Munch.

— What flavour?

— Beef.

— Beef? Forget it. I was gonna swap you, but not for cow.

Liam started to eat, his square face chewing his sandwich like a camel that was in a rush. Ryan smiled. Liam had been his best friend since the infants and he couldn't think of a single day since they'd known each other that Liam hadn't made him laugh at least twice.

— I heard you got caught watching the girls do PE.

As Liam spoke, little bits of sandwich flew out of his mouth on to the table.

— I wasn't watching the girls. Jeez, Liam, can you keep the food in your mouth?

Liam shrugged his thick shoulders.

— That's not what I heard. Tracey said Miss Zaidel properly got you and you went bright red and everything.

— Yeah, well, Tracey's full of it.

Liam peeled a banana and took half of it with one bite.

— You should just pick one.

— What?

— Pick one. Any girl – there's loads of them. Look, there's some.

Liam stuck out his big arm. Ryan slapped it down.

— What are you doing?

Liam pushed the last bit of banana into his mouth.

— I would just walk up to one of them and lay it down.

— Lay it down? What does that even mean? Just eat your food, man.

— I'm just saying I'd do that.

Ryan took another bite of his roll.

— You don't get it.

— What don't I get, Ryan? You choose one and then you lay it down.

— Stop saying that. And you don't just choose one, do you? It's not an auction.

Liam looked confused. Ryan finished the last of his roll.

— And you wouldn't lay it down anyway.

— Yeah I would. I'd lay it down hard.

— Oh really? Big Liam? Mr Smooth, yeah? And what would you say?

— Call me Big L.

— You're an idiot.

Liam slapped the banana skin on to the table and puffed up his chest.

— I'd walk straight up to her and be like, look, baby, it's me and you, yeah? You can be the I S P to this Big L. What you sayin'?

Ryan shook his head and smiled. Liam looked offended.

— What? That's good. Big L. I S P, lips, like kiss.

— That spells lisp, you idiot.

— What?

Ryan watched Liam's face as his brain worked out the spelling.

— Oh yeah. Yeah, well, you know what I mean.

— Yeah. Big L can't spell.

Liam smiled.

— Big L can't spell, but you smell, like beef, you've got cow crisps in your teeth.

His big fists started to knock a beat on the lunch table. Ryan smiled and tried to think of a comeback rhyme.

Ameliah watches the girls around the table talking about things everybody expects girls to talk about. Their fast lips motoring through sentences.

Heather gives her a look that says 'Stop being so quiet' and Ameliah tries to say with her eyes that she's only quiet when she's around people talking about things she doesn't care about, that she's not interested in the fact that Simone has taken some of her older sister's foundation and eyeliner and is going to do makeovers for people after school on the field. Mum always said that foundation was what you build houses on and, if your face needs to be built on, then make-up isn't really going to make a difference, is it?

But Heather already knows.

Ameliah looks at her. Pretty without trying. The freckles scattered across her nose and cheeks making her seem that little bit more special. Thank God for Heather. The bridge between her and the others. Heather knows how to let Ameliah be in the group without having to do or say too much. She's always done it, since the infants.

— You OK, Am? Half a day left then freedom.

Heather smiles. Ameliah smiles back. She thinks about the two of them sitting inside Dad's tent in her room by torchlight, Heather hiding her face in the neck of her jumper as Ameliah tells her Dad's ghost stories,

Heather screaming as she gets to the end and the big shock about the old man with no head.

— You wanna try it?

Heather holds out the little eyeliner pencil and smiles. Ameliah smiles back and Heather lowers her hand.

— I'm coming back to yours after school, right?

— Yeah?

— Yeah. We're gonna make a start on those boxes.

Ameliah looks around at the other girls, all engrossed in talk of makeovers and brush technique.

— We don't need to.

Heather reaches out for Ameliah's hand.

— Yes, we do. New summer chapter, Am. It's time to make it your room.

Ryan shook his head and tried to see straight. The warm pain in the back of his neck was starting to spread round towards his face. The football lay on the floor next to the front door of the house. He could feel grit in the palm of his hand as he sat up on the short front path. He looked up at Nathan standing over him, laughing, and felt a knot forming in his stomach.

26

— You should've ducked. I shouted duck. It's your own fault, weed, always daydreaming.

Nathan stepped over Ryan's legs and took out his key to open the door. Ryan got to his feet, the knot in his stomach growing and starting to move up inside his chest. He stared at Nathan's back and imagined doing some kind of flying karate kick, sending his stepbrother flying through the front door. The knot made its way up along his throat into his mouth, ready to scream.

Nathan pushed open the front door and disappeared inside. Ryan breathed deeply and swallowed the knot, feeling it melt into nothing in his throat.

Inside, Ryan sat down on the sofa in a spot where he could see out of the front window. The pain in the back of his neck had weakened to a dull ache. He rubbed his eyes with his knuckles and looked round the room.

He tried to remember before Nathan had moved in. Before Dad got together with Sophia. Before Mum.

He stared at the big rectangular mirror above the fireplace, its heavy wooden frame like something from an old castle. It looked completely out of place in the room, but had always been there. Sophia had tried to move it out when she moved in, saying it didn't belong there. Dad had got serious and said it was going nowhere, anything else could go, but the mirror stayed.

Ryan liked that Dad had said that. He knew the story. Mum had chosen the mirror when she and Dad first bought the house. It was really heavy and, as they carried it into the house, Dad had slipped and dropped his end and the mirror hit the floor but didn't break, and Mum said it was a sign of good luck. Mum believed in luck.

Ryan stared at the mirror and thought about how she loved old things and, even though he found it harder and harder to picture her face, he knew that the mirror was a connection to her.

A heavy thud hit the ceiling above his head. Ryan imagined Nathan falling off his bed or tripping over his stupid weights and lying flat out on the floor of what used to be Dad's office. He smiled to himself and waited for the sounds of his stepbrother getting up and stamping around, but nothing came, only quiet. Ryan's stomach dropped. He jumped to his feet and ran upstairs.

— Nathan! Are you OK?

He burst into the office, panicked. Nathan was on the floor in his pants and vest doing stomach crunches. Against the wall behind him, a Casio keyboard drum machine lay across a small desk next to a small black TV. He stopped and stared up at Ryan.

— What are you doing? What's wrong with you?

Ryan looked round the room. He saw a poster of the solar

system, a couple of footballers torn out of magazines and, on the right, one huge picture of Bruce Lee doing a high kick. On the floor, a plate held a half-eaten doorstop sandwich.

— I thought I heard a—

— A bang? And what? You thought I was hurt? Man, you're such a girl.

Nathan scoffed and carried on with his crunches. Ryan spotted a small bookcase behind the TV, full of science books. He felt his nose wrinkle up.

— Since when do you read about science?

Nathan sat up, his arms resting on his knees, and frowned.

— What? I can't be into science?

Ryan shrugged. Nathan shook his head.

— Ryan, I probably know more than you, I just don't have to be a weed with it.

He lowered his body back to the floor ready for more crunches.

— Now get lost, yeah?

Ryan backed out of the room and pulled the door to. He stood on the landing, listening to Nathan's grunts, and told himself the science books were just for show.

Ameliah and Heather stare at the machine. It's faded black, the silver panels battered and worn. The large clunky buttons look like they were designed by a toddler. The plastic of the little windows for the tape decks is cloudy with scratches.

— It looks like it should be in a museum or something.

Heather touches the chipped circular speaker on one side.

— How old is it?

Ameliah shrugs.

— I don't know. I found it in the spare room.

— Where your nan's keeping all that stuff?

— Yeah. I'm gonna go through it all.

— Maybe it's worth something? You see things like this on those TV shows.

Heather fiddles with the large silver tuning dial, making the tiny orange frequency indicator move left and right along the black strip.

— I mean it doesn't even have a CD thing. It's prehistoric.

— It's not for sale.

Ameliah picks up an old shoebox from the many that lie spread across the floor among black bags full of clothes and two old suitcases. The shoebox is packed full of cassette tapes, some with sleeves, some without.

— It plays these. There's boxes of them.

She pulls out one of the tapes and dusts the cover with her sleeve. *James Brown – Greatest Hits.* She feels herself smile.

— My mum used to go on about James Brown.

She hands it to Heather. Heather smiles.

— She loved music, right?

— Yeah. They both did. I used to hear them playing stuff and giggling through the wall.

— How cool would it have been if she'd been the music teacher at our school instead of what's-his-face?

Ameliah pictures Mum, sitting on the sofa covered in sheets of music, trying to plan her lessons.

— Yeah.

She taps her hand on the box of tapes.

— I'm gonna listen to them all.

Heather inspects the cassette in her hand like evidence at a crime scene.

— Why is it so big? Look, this one only has eleven tracks! Is he a rapper?

Ameliah runs her finger over the spines of the other

tapes in the box, wiping a clean line on the dusty plastic like a snowplough.

— They're all jumbled up now. Some of them are blanks, I think. You wanna listen to some?

Heather stands up.

— Nah. It's all so old, Am, it's gonna take you weeks to go through it all.

She drops the tape on to the bed and moves to one of the black bags. Ameliah stares at the tapes.

— Yeah, well, I've got six, haven't I?

— You can't spend the whole six weeks' holidays digging through dusty old stuff like a mole.

Ameliah smiles at Heather.

— A mole?

Heather nods.

— Yeah. A mole. A little scruffy blind mole scared of the sun.

Ameliah laughs.

— Shut up.

Heather smiles and starts going through a bin bag full of clothes.

— I wonder if any of this would fit you, you should—

— Leave it.

Ameliah's voice is sharp. Heather stops what she's doing. Ameliah looks down.

— Sorry, I mean I want to go through it myself, to start with I mean.

She looks up to where the ceiling meets the wall, noticing a thin crack running along the join. Heather walks over to her.

— It's OK. I get it.

Ameliah nods her head in the way she's perfected.

As Heather looks at the box of tapes, Ameliah pictures the spare room, along the landing, stacked ceiling-high with bags and boxes, and wonders how much everything Mum and Dad left behind would weigh.

Ryan felt every muscle in his body shaking from the pressure. He stared at the chocolate-brown carpet. This close up he could make out the individual fibres and it struck him how much they looked like the crop circles he'd read about in his *Book of the Unexplained*. He could feel his lungs pressing against the inside of his chest. He told himself that he had to do one more. If he could just do a second one, that wasn't so bad. Two press-ups was twice as many as the one he'd managed.

The one that had felt like it was going to kill him. He thought about Nathan sitting on top of him on the living-room floor. The feeling of knowing that even if he tried his hardest he wouldn't be able to push him off.

— Come on, weed. Do it!

But the effort of speaking the words seemed to drain the last bit of strength from his arms and Ryan collapsed, face down on the floor.

He lay there on his side. It didn't matter that he could only do one press-up. It wasn't like people hung out and just did press-ups, was it? In fact, what use was a press-up anyway? When would anyone ever be in a situation where they were trapped on their front and needed to push themselves up a little bit?

He thought about lying squashed under Nathan's backside, trying to turn his head so he could at least see the TV, feeling like Nathan weighed as much as a family saloon car. He closed his eyes, bent his elbows, pushed his palms flat into the chocolate crop-circle floor, filled his lungs and, with everything he had, pushed himself up until his arms were straight.

Downstairs, the front door closed and Ryan heard Dad's

familiar footsteps make their way into the living room. He lay back down on the floor with his ear pressed to the carpet. The muffled sounds of Sophia asking Dad about his day reminded Ryan of tuning the FM dial on his boom box and catching partial broadcasts of talk radio covered in static. Dad's voice was low and monotone. One horizontal line of sound. Sophia's voice moved up and down like a heart monitor, rising at the end of a sentence like everything was a question.

Ryan thought about how sound travels in a straight line and either bounces off or gets absorbed by anything it hits. How sound travels faster and further in water than in air. How blue whales can hear each other's calls from thousands of miles away. He thought about stethoscopes and his toy doctor's kit from when he was a little boy. How he'd gone round the house putting the chest piece on everything he could find, trying to hear what was inside.

He felt the blood rush from his head as he stood up and went over to the window.

Outside, the last of the sunlight cast a shadow of the house on to the narrow strip of back lawn. Ryan stared up to where the thin fence separated the top of their back garden and the bottom of the house's opposite. The fat smoky-grey cat that nobody owned was sitting motionless on top of the fence like some kind of furry gargoyle looking up at him. Ryan stared at it and imagined it suddenly spreading big bat-like wings and flying straight towards his window.

The living-room door closed downstairs and Ryan heard Dad start up the stairs. He quickly slipped into his desk chair and clicked on the little lamp, opening a dark blue exercise book and grabbing a pen.

The sound of the saxophone comes through the crackly speakers like lines of smoke, snaking their way up and around the walls.

Ameliah lies on her bed, staring at the cassette box in her hands. The blurred photograph on the front has a blueish tint and shows the man playing with his eyes closed, his cheeks puffed out with air. Above his head letters spell his name, John Coltrane.

Ameliah imagines Mum lying on her bed, like she is now, holding the same cassette box, listening to the same notes floating around her walls, closing her eyes like the man on the cover. She looks round the room. The old dark wardrobe almost reaches the ceiling; the door of the left-hand side has a long mirror set into it. Past the wardrobe, underneath the window, boxes and bags sit like they're outside a charity shop.

At the end of the bed on the left, the gloss white door is pushed almost closed, its four rectangular panels raised like Braille.

Ameliah looks at the tape in her hands.

— John Coltrane.

Her words seem to sit on top of the music for a second before melting away.

She looks at the old stereo and imagines its insides to be lots of tiny cogs, like a watch, its little motor working to turn the tapes around in time.

On the floor next to her bed, five shoeboxes full of cassette tapes each lie open, waiting to be heard. Another full box is next to her on the bed.

She hears Nan shutting the living-room door and starting up the stairs.

Ameliah reaches over and pushes the stop button.

The music cuts off and the room feels weirdly empty. The bedroom curtains are still open and the dark outside has turned the window into a dull mirror, reflecting back the room in the lamplight.

There's a tap and the door slowly opens. Nan pokes her head in.

— You all right, love?

Ameliah watches Nan's eyes take in the newly arranged room, her old eyes moving over the walls and furniture.

— I'm fine, Nan. You going to bed?

Nan stares at the old stereo and smiles.

— I certainly am. These bones need their rest.

She stretches slowly like a cat.

— And you should get some rest too, young lady. Tomorrow's the start of summer.

Ameliah runs her hand over the tapes in the box next to her. Nan nods at them.

— You've got your own personal library there. Your mum loved her music. I'm sure you'll find all kinds of treasure in that room.

She nods her head towards the back of the house and the spare room. Ameliah watches Nan remember something, some scene from her life with Mum, when Mum was young.

— I won't stay up too late, Nan.

Nan stares into space for a moment then cracks a

smile. She gives the room another once-over then speaks slowly.

— No. Not too late.

She slips out and closes the door.

Ameliah listens to Nan make her way along the landing to her room. Matching the pace of Nan's feet, she walks her fingertips over the spines of the cassettes in the open box. Nan reaches her room and the footsteps stop. Ameliah stops her fingers.

Nan's door closes and the house falls quiet. Ameliah pulls out the tape she arrived at. Its clear sleeveless case is foggy with scratches.

She opens the case, letting the old cassette slide out on to her chest. Holding it up to the lamplight, she can just about see through the battered plastic to the tape spools inside. She can see bumps along the dark spools that look like the tape has been stuck back together. The torn remains of a dirty label show the letter M, handwritten in dark blue ink.

She rolls over and opens tape deck two, easing the cassette in until she feels the click.

She pushes the tape deck closed, presses play and rolls on to her back, staring up.

The speakers hiss and a low scratching creeps out. Ameliah looks at the stereo.

The hiss carries on and is now joined by what sounds like wind moving between buildings. Ameliah props herself up with her elbow, looking at the speakers.

There's the sound of static and something like a short burst of popcorn cooking.

Ameliah screws up her face and reaches for the stop button and then she hears the voice.

Ryan spat white foam into the sink. He watched the stream of cold water carry the old toothpaste in a circle towards the plughole like sewage. He'd read that, on the equator, water just went straight down with no swirls, like there was no time to hang around.

Sophia's squeak of a laugh came through the floorboards.

Downstairs, her and Dad would be curled up on the sofa with their wine, watching their Friday night film.

Tilting his head, Ryan could hear the TV coming from Nathan's room across the landing, even through two closed doors.

He thought about earlier at dinner. All four of them sitting round the circular table like a rubbish version of King Arthur and his knights. Dad would be Arthur, which would make Sophia Guinevere. He would be Lancelot and Nathan would be some other rubbish knight with a short temper and poor sword skills.

Even now, months after they'd moved in, their sit-down dinners felt awkward. When Mum was alive, they'd never done it. With her and Dad working on the other side of town, it meant they didn't get back till late, so Ryan mostly sorted his own food out. The only time they ate together was on Sunday and that was in front of the TV watching *The Cosby Show*.

Sophia took dinner very seriously. Laying the table, having things in bowls with big spoons, and even napkins. It almost felt like a restaurant. Dad went along with it. He had sat Ryan down and told him he liked how different things felt. That if things were going to move on they had to feel new and that he knew Ryan understood that.

Sitting at the table watching Sophia and Dad smiling at each other as they passed the broccoli or poured each other more wine would've turned Ryan's stomach if it hadn't been for the look on Dad's face. Nathan hated it. He didn't say anything directly, but the way he spoke to Sophia and the little comments he'd make whenever Dad said something made it obvious to everyone. If Ryan was honest, part of the reason the meals were not completely unbearable was because, however uncomfortable he felt, he could always tell Nathan hated it more.

Ameliah quickly looks round the room. Her mouth open, her eyes narrowed, she strains to hear the words.

She sits up and shuffles herself towards her pillow, getting closer still to the speakers. A low hissing breathes out then:

— It's just weird, I mean since he showed up, I dunno.

More static. Ameliah stares through the tiny tape-deck window and sees the dark tape moving from one spool to the other.

She rubs her hands down over her face and shakes her head.

— There's nothing there.

But even as she speaks the words she can make out the voice again, poking through the crackle.

— It's different now, you know?

Ameliah can't fully tell if it's the voice of a girl or a boy, but it sounds young. She catches her reflection in the long mirror on the old wardrobe, her top teeth biting her full bottom lip.

The crackle seems to cough more words she can't make out then:

— I miss you.

She feels herself shiver. Who is speaking?

She turns the volume dial a little and static fades up. Like somebody scrunching up a newspaper right next to her ear. The voice seems to be speaking but in a murmur. She moves her face until her nose is almost touching the speaker. The crackle gets louder and then:

— Eve.

Ameliah sits upright, feeling the hair on her arms stand up.

She stares at the speaker. Its dark mesh chipped in places, showing the metal under the black. The static gets louder, drowning out the voice. Ameliah turns the dial, trying to save it, talking into the speaker.

— Hello? Come back. Hello?

But the voice has gone. The static dies down, leaving nothing but the low hissing of the speakers. She sees her own face in the mirror, confused and tired.

She reaches out and pushes the stop button. The

hissing cuts off. She looks again into the mirror. Her reflection stares back a frown.

She reaches for the marker pen on her bedside table, grabs the lid of the opened shoebox and scribbles words: since he showed up, it's different now, I miss you, Eve.

The black ink seeps into the old cardboard making the edges of her letters seem fuzzy. Ameliah stares at the words, feeling her eyes fighting to stay open.

She sighs and rolls on to her back, the shoebox lid still in her hand. Staring up at the ceiling, her head fills with questions.

Whose voice was it? What were they talking about? Since who showed up? And, most of all, why did they say Mum's name?

CHAPTER 2

Sunlight seeped through Ryan's closed eyelids. His whole body felt like a rock that hadn't moved since cavemen walked the earth, embedded into his mattress like a boy-shaped jewel. He could hear his own breathing.

— Is she naked?

Ryan sprang up from the waist and opened his eyes. Across the room, Liam filled his desk chair like some kind of Bond villain.

— Is she naked?

— What you doing?

— Answer the question, Mr Bond, was she naked?

— Who?

— The girly you were dreaming about.

— Shut up, man.

Ryan scratched his head.

— What time is it? How did you get in?

— Your mum let me in, I mean stepmum. Do you say stepmum? What do you call her?

Ryan swung his legs from under the covers and rubbed his eyes.

— Sophia.

Liam's eyes scanned the room.

— Course. Sophia. She seems nice.

Ryan scratched his stomach through his Chicago Bears T-shirt.

— She's fine. Why are you here again?

— It's Saturday, Ryan. First day of the summer holidays. We've got stuff to do!

— What stuff?

Liam stared into space, looking for an answer.

— Good stuff. Get up, man.

He pushed himself out of the chair and walked over towards Ryan's bed. His baggy jeans and thick grey hoody made his body look like a man's.

Large movie posters and smaller pages cut from magazines peppered the light blue walls.

Liam stared at a poster showing a white-haired man in a lab coat and a younger man wearing a body warmer both looking at their watches in amazement, the words *Back to The Future II* emblazoned across the top in flame–coloured angled letters.

Liam opened his eyes wide and spun on his heels, pointing a finger at Ryan.

— Great Scott!! Six weeks off!!

Ryan looked up at him, frozen in his shocked pose.

He thought about how Liam had pretty much talked the whole way through any movie they had ever watched together. How he often asked the same question more than twice, seemingly having not much grasp of what was happening, and yet always ended up loving every movie they saw. When they'd watched *Batman* on video at Liam's house, Ryan had spent each scene having to go through every character saying whether they knew *Batman* was Bruce Wayne or not, even though only Alfred did.

Ryan jumped to his feet and grabbed Liam's outstretched finger.

— 1.21 jiggawatts?!

The pair of them laughed. Ryan moved to the windowsill and pulled a cassette from the full black plastic tape rack. He moved back to his bedside table, slotted the cassette into the boom box, turned up the volume, pressed play, then, lifting one hand and extending his index finger, he mimed along with the opening words.

The sound of scratching then the track started. Ryan and Liam began to bounce along with the beat, shuffling their feet on the carpet, bending at the waist, slowly punching the air in time as the female voice sang the chorus to *Summertime* by DJ Jazzy Jeff & The Fresh Prince.

The pair of them heard something at the same time. Ryan turned down the volume just as Nathan burst into the room, his chest puffed up.

— You better turn that rubbish—

Nathan looked at Liam, surprised to find someone else in the room. Liam looked at Ryan. Ryan glanced at Nathan then looked down. Liam stared at Nathan. Nathan's chest seemed to deflate.

— Yeah, well, I don't know why you listen to that stuff anyway.

Liam's eyes never left Nathan.

— Because we like it.

Nathan looked at Ryan.

— What's he even doing in your room this early? Did you two have a little sleepover or something?

Ryan looked at Liam. Liam smiled then turned to Nathan.

— Yeah. We did. We had a sleepover and did each other's make-up and talked about kittens. What's your problem?

He stepped forward. Nathan moved back into the doorway, reaching for the handle.

— Yeah, well, you two lovebirds have fun doing each other's hair.

He backed out of the room, his eyes moving between them

both. Liam stared him out the whole way. As the door closed, the cassette tape finished and the play button clicked off. Liam looked at Ryan.

Ryan frowned.

— Kittens?

Liam shrugged his shoulders.

— I don't know, do I? I was freestyling.

— Yeah, but kittens?

— Yeah, fluffy ones, with big eyes. Is he always such a knob?

Ryan opened a white drawer at the bottom of the wardrobe and pulled out a large navy blue T-shirt.

— Pretty much. So what are we doing?

Liam flopped down on to the unmade bed, his arms spread out and stretching over the sides.

— Everyone'll probably be in the park.

Ryan dropped his Bears T-shirt on the floor and pulled his head through the clean one. The end of the dark sleeves reached past his elbow.

— All right, but can we ride through the woods first?

Liam sat up and smiled.

— If you can keep up.

The light tan A4 envelope is creased from being rolled up. Written in untidy writing across the top right-hand corner are the words Personal Effects. Ameliah reaches her hand inside and pulls out a small moulded keyring. The clear plastic holds a green four-leaf clover against a white background. She runs her thumb over its smoothness. A window-shaped rectangle of sunlight sits on the deep red bedroom carpet. Through the floorboards Nan sings along to Nina Simone.

Ameliah turns the keyring over in her fingertips. One deep scratch cuts diagonally across it, blurring the words 'The luck of the Irish'.

She runs her thumb along the scratch, pressing her nail into the gouged-out valley.

Downstairs, Nan struggles with a high note. Ameliah lays the keyring on the bed and reaches back into the envelope, pulling out a small pearl-coloured shell. Roughly the size of a fifty-pence piece, it sits like a miniature fan in the palm of her hand, thin grooves running from the curved edge towards what would be the fan's handle. Just in from the edge a small perfectly round hole has been drilled, where the thread used to be. Ameliah touches the shell with her fingertip. She thinks about it against Mum's skin. The creamy white catching the light around her neck on its black string.

— Am!

Nan's voice comes through the floor. Ameliah slips the shell into her pocket then her hand back into the envelope. The small mobile phone looks out of date but brand new. The charcoal-coloured plastic unscratched, its smooth lifeless screen framed in silver metal.

She holds the phone carefully, tracing the small dark buttons with her fingertips.

— Ameliah! I thought you were meeting your friends?

Nan is calling over the music from the bottom of the stairs. Ameliah slips the phone back in, then the keyring, and folds the envelope in half. As she pushes it underneath her pillow, her eyes catch the dark letters on the shoebox lid. She stares at Mum's name written in block capitals. Her fingers feel the smooth shell in her pocket as she stares at the old stereo.

— The universe.

Her words hang in the air and for a second she's not sure whether she actually said them out loud.

— Ameliah! I'm leaving now!

Ameliah closes her eyes and inhales deeply.

— I'm coming!

Ryan planted one foot and spun the back wheel of his BMX behind him, leaving the perfect arc of a skid. Dust from the ground floated up, caught in the tractor beams of light cutting through the high canopy of the tall trees.

Liam hit his back brake, leaving a long straight line in the ground, stopping right beside Ryan. The pair of them looked out beyond the edge of the trees, where the noise of voices let them know the park was already packed.

— Mary might be here.

Liam's voice travelled up in the open space.

— She might give us money for chips.

Mary was in the year above, but was always nice to Ryan. At school people knew not to mess with her and, as far as big sisters went, he always thought Liam dropped lucky.

— She likes you. Smile at her and we might get enough for a scallop as well.

Liam digged Ryan in the arm and rode off towards the noise.

Ryan felt the warm burn of his arm going numb and, even though nobody could see him, he pretended it didn't hurt.

Groups of kids huddled together in different-size packs, some standing, some sitting as the sun moved into the afternoon side of the sky. A few stray kids sat in pairs or threes with the odd individual flitting back and forth between groups like a carrier pigeon.

Ryan stared out across the wide stretch of green and imagined that from above they all looked like a game of Risk in full flow.

Over to the right, he made out Nathan involved in a football game with too many players. He looked across at Liam who was scanning the area for his sister.

— It's like the Serengeti.

Liam was busy focusing, moving over faces and frames like the Terminator.

— Where is she?

Ryan saw Nathan slide into a tackle with a boy with long blond hair, sending him up into the air before crashing on to the floor. Nathan got up and carried on with the game, leaving the blond boy in a crumpled heap.

— Just the lions and the gazelle.

Liam looked at him.

— What are you talking about?

Ryan made out a circle of girls from the year above over to their right.

— Doesn't matter. There's Mary.

As they approached the group of girls, pushing their bikes, Ryan felt his stomach tighten as his mind turned the group into a pride of lionesses, stretched out in the sun, all capable of killing him with one swipe.

He slowed his stride down slightly so that Liam was clearly leading, hoping that would mean he could ride out the whole encounter without having to speak.

Mary was sitting with her back facing them. Her strong arms propping up her body, her dark hair cropped above her neck. Liam nudged Ryan.

— Just play it cool, yeah? And don't forget to smile. I want that scallop.

Ryan wasn't listening to Liam, his ears had picked up on a voice. A girl's voice, with an accent that made his head swim.

An accent he hadn't heard for what felt like ages. An accent that felt like home.

The sounds of the park seemed to go underwater as she looked up, her green eyes staring straight at him.

Liam mumbled as Mary handed him something. Ryan stared at

the girl. He could feel the blood in his hands as his fingers tightened round his handlebars.

— Come on, Spanner.

Liam's backhand across his chest brought him crashing back. The noise of the park seemed even louder than before as Liam pulled him by the arm. All around them other kids carried on.

Ryan felt light as Liam led him away.

— What happened to you smiling at her? She only gave me a quid.

Ryan turned his head as they walked, trying to get another look at the girl, but the circle had closed up and she was out of sight.

— Who was she?

Liam threw his leg over his seat.

— Who?

— The girl. The one next to your sister. With the dark hair. Did you see her?

— I didn't see anything, except you ruin our chance of a scallop.

Ryan stared into space.

— She was Irish. Why was she Irish?

He smiled to himself. Liam looked at the small gold coin in his shovel hand.

— Who cares? Why are you such a flop? We're gonna have to share a bag now. Forget this, let's go to Allsports and look at the trainers.

Ryan nodded but wasn't listening. As he climbed on to his bike and they rode away, all he could hear was her voice.

Ameliah rubs sleep from her eyes with her knuckles as she cuts across the grass towards the little kids' playground. She feels warm in her grey hoody hanging over the waist of her jeans, the edge of her dark curls poking out from the hood. The high sun bounces off the climbing frames, making her squint.

A group of young mums chase toddlers round the slide like chickens. On the other side of the playground a band of girls sits at a dark wooden bench wearing different colour combinations of the same denim leggings and vest top outfit. Ameliah makes out Heather, her hands moving quickly in front of her, like a conductor leading the conversation.

Beyond the girls the smooth cream bowl of the small skate park is busy with boys trying hard to look cool.

Ameliah looks at her watch. It's two o'clock.

— Am!

Heather's voice booms across the park. The other girls at the table look round. The young mums and their toddlers all turn towards Heather like meerkats.

— Ameliah!

Heather is standing up, waving her arm. Ameliah smiles. Heather beams back. The other girls shake their heads as Heather sits down, moving along to make space on the bench.

Ameliah hears the auto-tuned voice of some pop star among the park sounds. As she approaches the bench, she sees a sleek touch-screen mobile phone resting on the grainy dark wooden table. The voice is spiking out from its tinny speakers.

She climbs on to the bench, feeling all eyes on her, as though her arrival has pressed pause on the conversation. Heather puts her arm round her shoulder.

— You look half asleep, Am. You stay up too late?

Ameliah hears the voice on the tape in her head. She rubs her eyes again and nods.

— I got distracted.

Heather smiles.

— By that old machine?

— Yeah.

Heather turns to the others.

— You lot should see the stereo Am found. It's crazy. Like older than us, it's got these massive buttons.

The other girls watch, but are clearly not listening. Ameliah sees Simone's face change as she brushes one side of her jet-black hair over her shoulder and stares past her, smiling. Turning to look behind her, Ameliah sees three older boys walking side by side, a stone's throw away, towards the exit near the main road. All three of them are wearing coats too big for the weather and New Era caps that hide the top halves of their heads.

Ameliah stares at the boy on the side nearest to her. She can make out sharp cheekbones. The line of jet-black hair against the pale skin of his neck. Something about the way he moves makes him stand out from the other two, like his feet barely need to touch the ground, the bottom edge of his charcoal tracksuit bottoms almost swallowing his trainers.

— There he is. How fine is he?

Simone's voice is excited. Ameliah turns back to

look at her. The other girls all nod as they stare at the boys. Simone stands up.

— Hey!

Her voice sounds out like a car alarm. Ameliah turns back to the boys, who are now almost at the exit. All three of them look back and Ameliah sees his face. His dark eyes stare straight at her. She feels her chin retreating into her hoody, but her eyes never leave him. She watches his head tilt slightly, as though he's trying to place her.

The biggest of the three boys slaps his shoulder and they all walk through the gap in the fence and away down the road.

Ameliah turns back round slowly, feeling a warmth in her stomach. Simone smiles cockily.

— You see him look at me?

She sits back down.

— He's a lot. He wants me, I can tell.

The other girls seem to congratulate her with their eyes. Ameliah stares into her lap.

Simone looks at her.

— He was in my cousin's year. I think he works at the supermarket.

— What's his name?

Simone glances at Heather then back at Ameliah and smiles.

— Why, Am? You like him?

Ameliah avoids her eyes. Simone scoffs.

— Ha, you do!

Ameliah feels the others staring. Heather nudges her elbow.

— He was nice, Am.

— Ameliah likes a boy!

Simone's voice cuts into Ameliah's ears as she looks up.

— No offence, Am, but I think you might be aiming a bit high. He's clearly into me.

Reaching for her phone, she strokes the screen with her slender thumb. Ameliah's fingers squeeze the shell in her jeans pocket as she watches Simone scroll through her playlist.

— Where you been anyway? she asks Ameliah. Didn't you get the text?

Simone doesn't look up. Ameliah looks at Heather. Heather nods.

— She doesn't have a mobile.

The other girls tilt their heads in unison like confused pigeons. Ameliah adjusts herself in her seat.

— I do have one. I just don't really use it.

She frowns at Heather. Heather bites her lip

— Yeah. That's what I meant. It's always on silent, right?

Simone taps her phone screen and another track starts with the same auto-tuned voice. She lays the phone back down on the table.

— Aren't you hot in that big thing?

Ameliah peels her hood from her head, freeing her curls.

— Not really.

Heather cuts in.

— Help me out, Am. These lot reckon that mind-reading is real. It's not real, is it?

The other girls shake their heads, shrugging their shoulders. Simone wags her finger.

— I didn't say mind-reading, Heather, did I? I was talking about psychics, like mediums and that. My mum went to one, she said it was a tiny little basement place, near the sea, and this woman told her she could contact people and they spoke to her great aunty or uncle or whatever.

A girl with mousy brown hair pulled back in a tight ponytail joins in.

— Yeah, and my dad said him and his mates did one of them Ouija board things when they were at school and it proper moved and everything!

Heather sighs through a smile.

— It's all tricks, isn't it, Am? Tell them. Nobody hears voices from the other side. *Ooooooooh!*

She waves her hands in front of her and does her best rubbish ghost impression.

Ameliah scans the other girls. Her fingertips turn the shell round and round in her pocket. Simone stares at her. She glances at Heather. High above them the sun moves behind a cloud.

— I dunno.

Heather stops being a ghost and looks at her.

— What?

Ameliah shrugs.

— I dunno. Some people believe in it.

Simone looks angry.

— What do you mean some people?

Ameliah stares back at Simone.

— I mean some people, they believe it.

Simone's frown deepens.

— Some people like who?

Her voice sharpens. Ameliah hears the voice from the tape in her head saying Mum's name.

— Like my dad.

The other girls stare at her. Heather looks shocked.

— Am?

Ameliah looks at Heather, feeling Simone watching her.

— My dad said he heard a voice once. When he was a boy. He said the voice of a girl spoke to him. That it helped him.

Simone looks at Heather.

— See. Even Ameliah knows about it.

Heather scrunches up her face and shakes her head.

— Are you serious, Am? You never told me that.

Ameliah shrugs.

— Yeah, I mean it wasn't a big deal or anything. I don't think he thought he was talking to the dead, it was probably just a story he told me. He told lots of stories.

Heather puffs out her cheeks.

— All right, great. Stories, mediums, psychos.

Simone cuts in.

— Psychics, Heather, not psychos.

— Whatever.

Heather pulls a small white paper bag out of the large pocket at the front of her hoody.

— Who wants one?

Her fingers reach into the bag and pull out a deep red sweet. Simone looks at the bag.

— What's in there?

Heather pops the sweet into her mouth.

— Wine gums. My mum brought loads home.

The other girls look at the bag then at her.

— Help yourself.

Five painted fingernailed hands dive at the bag, tearing it open, grabbing the coloured sweets. The sun moves from behind the cloud and light bounces off the flat phone screen. Heather looks at Ameliah and shakes her head. Ameliah shrugs. Simone speaks as she chews.

— These are so bad for your teeth, Heather, and I heard they've got pig fat in them.

Heather looks down.

— Yeah, and cow nipples and sheep toes.

She lifts her head, pulling a smiling monster face, her teeth peppered with chewed pieces of sweet. Simone recoils.

— You're disgusting, Heather.

The other girls lean back in their seats.

Heather smiles wider and a piece of sweet drops out of her mouth. Simone and the other girls jump out of their seats, squealing.

— Stop it, Heather! That's so gross!

Heather stands up and starts moving towards Simone. The girls scatter, all cackling like animals. Ameliah smiles, holding the shell in her pocket, and stares at the empty gate that the boys left through as Heather stomps after the others.

— Just leave it to me.

Liam pushed four thick chips into his mouth at once, blowing out steam from the hot potato as he and Ryan sat next to each other on the low stone wall outside the chip shop, their bikes lying at their feet.

Ryan blew on a chip in his right hand, holding the bag they were sharing in his left. Liam reached into the wrapped-up newspaper and pulled out another hot handful.

— I'll be real smooth with it too.

He filled his mouth with chips. Ryan looked serious.

— Please, Liam. Promise me you won't mess this up.

Liam spoke through hot chewed potato.

— Relax, man. I'll speak to Mary later. I'll be so undercover, she won't even realise she's feeding me information.

— Just the basics. Name, where she came from, what she's doing here.

Ryan bit into his chip. Liam swallowed and nodded.

— I understand, man. I'll get you the information you need.

His eyes narrowed as he smiled.

— Juz mek shoo you av ze micro film, Meester Bond.

— I'm serious, Liam.

Liam took more chips.

— All right, all right, chill out, will ya? I'll find out who she is. You know this could've all been avoided if you'd just spoken to her.

— And you'll ring me later?

Liam rolled his eyes and spoke through a full mouth.

— Yes, I'll ring you later with my report. Jeez, can we leave it now?

The pair of them sat eating in silence as the low sun cast shadows of the houses opposite into the road. Ryan thought about the girl, her green eyes looking straight at him.

— Before nine though, yeah? I can't answer the phone after—

— Ryan, just relax.

Liam took the bag from Ryan's hand, dug out the last couple of chips then scrunched up the paper into a greasy ball and smiled.

— Just leave it to Big L.

Ameliah smells food as she shuts the front door. She can hear the TV through the wall. The windowless hallway is early evening dark. Her stomach rumbles and she realises that none of the girls even mentioned eating. She stops in front of the small oval mirror above the phone table and smiles, proud of herself for lasting so long with them.

Her thumb strokes the smooth inside of the shell in her pocket, warm from a day of being held. The finger-like leaves of the spider plant next to the phone reach over the handset and, as she opens the living-room door, she wonders how something can survive with so little light.

Nan is sitting on the pale green sofa, knees tucked under her, holding a floral cushion in her lap. Light from the TV washes the room, reflecting in her eyes. On the screen a clunky-looking cowboy points a gun at a younger man on the floor.

— Hi.

Nan's eyes don't leave the screen.

— Hello, love. How was your day?

Ameliah shrugs.

— OK thanks. How about you?

Nan winces as the clunky cowboy shoots a warning shot at the ground next to the younger man's hand.

— Yes, fine, love. Dinner's almost ready. I hope you're hungry.

She brings her balled-up fist to her mouth as the younger man reaches for the gun and the clunky cowboy shoots him dead. Ameliah looks at the old TV, its heavy silver body framing the screen. The cowboy mounts his horse and starts to ride away. Ameliah stares at the framed photographs on top of the TV. Mum stares back at her, in her university robes.

— They don't make 'em like they used to.

Nan breathes out a sigh as she speaks. Ameliah watches as yellow letters spelling 'The End' roll up the screen.

— Good film?

Nan smiles.

— John Wayne.

Ameliah looks blank. Nan stares at her.

— The actor?

Ameliah shakes her head. Nan's mouth drops.

— You don't know who John Wayne is?

Ameliah shrugs.

— A cowboy?

Nan shakes her head.

— I bet that's your mum's doing. She always used to moan when I put a bit of John on.

Ameliah looks at her.

— She didn't like him?

Nan smiles.

— No, love, she didn't, which is why I'm guessing you've never seen him.

Ameliah looks down. The deep cream carpet changes colour as the TV moves to an advert.

— Which is just the perfect excuse for me to watch all his films again and educate you on the classics, isn't it?

Nan smiles, making a gun with two fingers, and mimes shooting Ameliah then blows imaginary smoke from her fingertips. Ameliah doesn't move. Nan pushes herself up to standing.

— Looks like we're going to have to work on your reactions too, kid.

She pats Ameliah on the shoulder.

— Come on. Let's have some chicken.

Ryan stared at the phone, the dark circular number buttons sticking out from deep red moulded plastic. The cord connecting it to the wall was stretched to where he sat halfway up the stairs. The upstairs landing light was on, but he'd left downstairs off so only the top half of his body was lit.

His bare feet tapped the edge of the stair excitedly in the dark. He could hear the TV in the living room through the wall. He thought about telekinesis and how Mum said we only use a fraction of our brain's capacity. Holding his fingertips against his temples, Ryan narrowed his eyes, focusing on the phone.

The ring boomed out. Ryan jumped and lost his footing, sliding down on his back to the bottom of the stairs. He sprang up, feeling the skin on his back burning as he dived towards the phone, picking up the receiver just as the living-room door opened.

— Hello? Yeah, it's me. Nothing. I just fell, hold on.

Nathan stood at the bottom of the stairs in dark shorts and T-shirt, holding a mug. Ryan cupped his hand over the receiver and stared at him.

— I'm on the phone.

Nathan sipped from his mug and smiled an evil smile.

— Yeah? And?

Ryan thought quickly.

— It's Liam.

Nathan's face changed. He cut his eyes at Ryan.

— Yeah, well, hurry up. My dad's calling at eight so you better be off. Enjoy your pillow talk, bumboy.

Ryan waited until the living-room door closed before moving the receiver to his mouth.

— Sorry, man. Yeah, it was Nathan. I swear down, one time I'll, what? I dunno. Cos he's a knob. Anyway, what did you find out? What do you mean? Nothing? At all?

Ryan's chest deflated. He rested his head in his hand, his elbow on his knee, then suddenly sat bolt upright.

— Don't do that! Seriously, man, it's not nice. Tell me, tell me. Yeah. Yeah. Just for the summer? Where from? OK. It doesn't matter. So she's in Mary's year? Right and what's her name? Stop it, Liam, just tell me.

Ryan laughed.

— Yo, you're lying. You are. Stop it, man, her name is not Esmeralda, come on. Of course I knew you were joking, now tell me her real name. Yeah. Really? Like from the bible?

I remember the three of us in the car cruising along a narrow road in Ireland. Me scared because it didn't seem like the road was made wide enough for two cars. Green fields stretching out on either side of us like a painting. Me spread across the back seat feeling glad I didn't have to share it with anyone, Dad driving while you navigated with the map. You remember? On our way to Blarney Castle to kiss a lucky stone.

How old was I, nine? Yeah, nine.

I didn't want to kiss it, did I? I said I didn't care about luck if it meant I had to kiss a dirty old stone. Dad glancing at you and smiling. Your fingers touching your necklace and you saying that it was luck that made me. Me rolling my eyes, knowing that I was going to hear the Mum and Dad and the universe fairy-tale story again. I heard that so many times, Mum.

The pair of you holding hands as Dad drove. I always thought that everybody's parents must have a fairy-tale story too, like that was how people ended up together. Magical moments that become stories you bore your children with.

I know different now.

The universe.

Remember the man who sat there all day holding people over the edge? His old smiley face, dark red and full of cracks. His rough hands on my back as he held me nearly upside down over the castle turret so I could kiss the cold slab thing. I remember closing my eyes and craning my neck to reach it and thinking about you both, holding hands, for a split second then, as I felt the cold stone on my lips, I thought about how many strangers' mouths must have touched it, and whether they got the luck they wished for.

I chose the keyring from the little gift shop with the four-leaf clover pressed inside, remember? The one I gave you? I remember I asked you if it was real. You looked at Dad and then at me and said that the only things that are real are the things we believe.

CHAPTER 3

The double-decker bus pulls into a stop on the main road towards town. Semi-detached houses stretch along either side. Ameliah sits, her knees up against the hand railing, resting her head against the upstairs window, staring out. She can feel the shell in her hip pocket, pressed against her thigh by the taut denim.

Heather sits next to her, head down, her thumbs speedily tapping her phone screen.

The top deck is empty except for a young suited man in the back corner behind them.

— Simone says they'll be outside Selfridges at twelve.

Her thumbs don't stop as she speaks. Ameliah stares out of the window. On the opposite side of the road she sees a skinny man wrestling with fitting a baby seat into a dirty white car. As the bus moves past, she sees the man taking a deep breath to compose himself.

— Am. Are you listening?

Ameliah smiles, seeing the skinny man kick his car door in frustration, just as he moves out of sight.

— You wanna meet them?

Heather's eyes flit between her phone screen and Ameliah. Ameliah nods.

— OK.

— Good. I say we go trying stuff on and then meet them later. Yeah?

She presses send and turns her phone over in her lap. Ameliah looks around the empty deck. In front of them a small flat screen shows the view of the bus's CCTV cameras on a rotating loop. She sees the young man from behind them in the screen. He sits alone, biting his nails. Ameliah nudges Heather and whispers.

— What do you reckon his name is?

Heather looks at the screen. The shot from the downstairs camera shows seats full of pairs of old people, most of them cradling chequered shopping bags.

— Who?

— Wait for it. It'll come back round in a minute. Keep your voice down.

The screen cuts to an image of Heather and Ameliah staring ahead as though they're looking for something. They both laugh. Heather combs her hair with her fingers.

— God, I look like a scarecrow or something.

Ameliah watches herself watching her best friend fixing her hair on the screen. Heather stares at the camera and pouts.

— We should have our own TV show.

The image changes to the view of the young man. Ameliah grabs Heather's hand.

Heather stares at the screen. The young man is picking his nose.

— *Euuuurgh.*

Ameliah squeezes Heather's hand.

— Sssshhhhhhh. He's behind us.

Heather looks over her shoulder. The man quickly lowers his hand from his face.

The image cuts to the old people downstairs. Ameliah fights a smile.

— I can't believe you.

Heather pushes her knuckle up into her nostril as though struggling with something stuck up there.

— Help me, Am, it's a big one.

Ameliah smiles.

— Stop it.

Heather carries on. Wrestling with her own hand in front of her face.

— *Mama mia!* This is huge, I think it might be—

Ameliah slaps Heather's hand down, pursing her lips as the young man moves past them, gripping the chair poles like he's swinging from vines in a tree. The bus slows as it approaches another stop. Both girls struggle to keep a straight face. The man avoids their eyes as he disappears down the stairs.

They both burst into laughter.

Heather's phone pings with the sound of a new message. She reads the screen as Ameliah wipes the corners of her eyes.

— I can't believe you.

Heather smiles.

— Yes you can. Look, Simone says there's some stall by the fountain giving away free health bars. We should go there first.

She holds the phone up to Ameliah. Ameliah nods her OK. Heather looks out of the window.

— It's weird being out on a Monday, isn't it? Feels like we're bunking or something.

Ameliah watches the houses outside turn to office blocks as they approach town.

— That's what school does to you. It takes time to adjust. We're programmed.

— All right, don't start getting all deep. We're going shopping, let's try and have fun, yeah?

Ameliah stares up through the glass at the new tall buildings as Heather's thumbs dance out a reply on her phone screen. Heather doesn't look up as she carries on speaking.

— I can hear your brain working you know.

Ameliah looks at her.

— Like a little machine, ticky-tick-ticking. Your room full of old stuff will still be there later. You can come with me for a day and pretend to be a girl, I mean, you know what I mean.

Ameliah stares at Heather.

— Don't look at me like that, Am. I just want us to have fun.

Ameliah bats her eyelids dramatically and presses her palms together.

— Maybe I'll find a miniskirt.

Heather bites her bottom lip and pinches Ameliah on the arm. Ameliah yelps. Heather nods.

— Yeah. That's what you get. Come on, this is our stop.

The familiar nasal voice came out from the boom box speakers. Ryan sat on his bedroom floor, knees bent, his back against his bed. In his lap an A4 pad of yellow lined paper held three chunky block letters. He scribbled, shading along the edge of an E with his biro as the high strings played out.

From where he sat, the window framed a clean blue rectangle of morning sky.

Ryan looked at his boom box as the strings plucked to signal the start of the beat. He lifted his pen just in time to strike his pad with the first hit of the drums as they kicked in. He nodded his head, tapping the block letters with his pen tip as the *boom bap* filled the room. He felt the blood running through his body as the liquid electric guitar riff ran under Q-Tip's spoken hook about Bonita Applebum.

Ryan stared at the page in front of him and smiled. His tapping pen tip had made speckles of blue ink across the last E of the word EVE.

He closed his eyes, letting himself float on top of the track. He pictured him and Liam approaching the circle of girls in the park. The back of Mary's head as they got closer. The sun on his back.

He opened his eyes, reaching up with his hand, and clicked the stop button on the boom box. The track cut off and the room fell silent. Ryan smiled and closed his eyes again, not wanting any background noise as his mind replayed her voice.

— Why are there so many people?

Ameliah stares up at the different levels of the shopping centre. Crowds of people move along, in and out of shops, to the sound of nondescript background music. Sunlight streams through the high glass ceiling. To their right, large escalators carry people between floors.

— It's like one of those experiments, with the mice.

She looks at Heather who is staring into the front window of a shoe shop eating a health bar.

— Don't you think?

Heather presses the fingertip of her free hand to the glass.

— There they are. Those are the ones. Aren't they gorgeous?

Ameliah follows the line of Heather's finger to a pair of light pink ballerina pumps.

— The girly girl slippers?

— No. Underneath. The Vans. I want them so bad.

Ameliah looks at Heather's feet. A pair of spotless white Vans hold fat double knots.

— Heather, you're wearing Vans.

Heather looks at Ameliah, rolling her eyes.

— You can never have too many Vans, Am.

She looks down at Ameliah's battered Converse.

— Maybe it's time you joined the club.

Ameliah traces a circle on the lacquered floor with her toes.

— I'm fine with these thanks. Can we go to the bookshop now?

Heather turns round, stretching out her arms towards the crowd of people moving past glass shopfronts.

— Look at all this! And you want to go and look at books?

A toddler waddles past them like a penguin, straining at a cord attached to his mother's hand. Heather watches him. Ameliah looks at the woman. The woman notices her watching and mimics being dragged along.

— Walkies!

Her voice is deeper than her face suggests and Ameliah and Heather look at each other surprised as the boy drags his mother towards the Early Learning Centre.

— Come on. We're supposed to meet them in a bit and we haven't even tried anything on yet.

As the pair of them step on to the upwards escalator, Ameliah puffs out her cheeks, blowing a fart sound out as she exhales. Heather shakes her head smiling.

— Didn't you used to go shopping with your mum?

Ameliah tries to remember any shopping trips with Mum as she stares at her smooth fingers holding the jet-black hand rail.

— Yeah, of course, I mean we must've done. I'm just not very good at it.

Heather pokes her in the arm.

— Well, I can help fix that. It'll be like in a film

where there's loads of clips of us trying stuff on while a song plays.

Ameliah looks at Heather.

— Montage.

— What?

As she opens her mouth to explain, she sees a man behind a young couple coming down on the busy escalator parallel to theirs. She recognises him but can't place him in her mind. A dirty-blond nest of thick hair on his head, his face somehow old and young at the same time. Handsome but in a scruffy kind of way. He looks at least as old as a teacher. He stares straight ahead, not noticing her watching him as they cross in opposite diagonal directions. Ameliah stares at the back of his head and his sharp shoulders under his dark green T-shirt. There's something about his face that makes her think of Mum and she can't work out why.

— You OK?

Heather cranes her neck to try and see what Ameliah is looking at.

— That guy.

— Which guy?

— The one with the scruffy hair, in the green T-shirt.

Heather scans the downwards escalator.

— I don't see any green T-shirt. Who was he?

Ameliah tries to place the man as he disappears out of sight.

— I dunno. He just looked familiar.

— Was he cute?

— Where do I know him from?

— Was he cute? I didn't see him. How old?

They step off the escalator and move round along the glass barrier. Ameliah stares down to the level below, trying to find the man in the crowd.

Heather stands next to her looking down.

— Has he gone? How old was he?

Ameliah scans the tops of people's heads.

— I dunno, thirty something?

Heather scrunches up her face.

— Thirty! What are you looking at old men for?

Ameliah gives up and turns round.

— I recognise his face, I just can't think where from. But it's like... I don't know. Like it's not a good memory.

Heather shakes her head.

— Forget the old man. Let's try some stuff on, please? This is supposed to be fun, Am.

Ameliah looks at Heather. Heather sticks out her bottom lip and gives her puppy-dog eyes. Ameliah smiles.

— OK. OK. Let's do your montage.

Heather's face straightens as Ameliah walks away.

— What's a montage?

The small flat stone skipped on top of the water four times before dropping through the surface. Liam punched a big fist in the air.

— Four times, *suckaaaaaaaaaa*!

Ryan sat on a thick tree root next to his bike and watched his best friend do an uncoordinated shuffle of celebration next to the edge of the stream.

On the other side of the water, tall light green reeds ran along in both directions. Beyond them an empty field stretched away towards an old farmhouse.

— How far do you think we rode?

Liam pulled at a thick branch above his head. The wood

creaked as it arched under his weight.

— I dunno. What time is it, three? We must've been riding at least an hour.

He looked around them.

— I don't even know where we are.

Ryan dug at the dirt with his heel and stared downstream.

— I didn't even see a bus stop.

Liam let go of the branch, sending it snapping up into the one above it. Twigs rained down on them both.

— It doesn't matter. All we do is ride back the way we came, right?

Ryan brushed a twig off his shoulder.

— Yeah.

He spotted a flat stone by his foot and picked it up, rubbing away the dirt with his fingers.

— You think she likes music?

He stood up and moved towards the edge of the water. Liam shrugged.

— Who doesn't like music?

— I mean our kind of music.

He shifted his feet, ready to throw the stone. Liam cleaned his earhole with his finger.

— I don't know. I told you what Mary said. I couldn't find out any more without looking obvious. Why does that matter anyway?

Ryan gripped the stone and tilted his head.

— I bet she does.

He flung his arm forward, snapping his wrist, sending the stone skimming across the top of the water. Both of them counted six bounces before the stone sank. Liam wrinkled his nose.

— You're just lucky.

He pulled his finger out of his ear and looked at his fingertip. Ryan took a bow.

— Yeah, right. Lucky. Again.

As he tried to straighten up his body, he felt weight pressing on the back of his neck. Liam's hand squeezed on the pressure points behind his ears. Ryan winced.

— OK. OK. Enough, man.

Liam released him. Ryan felt the blood in his face as he stood up straight. He scowled at Liam. Liam smiled and waved a finger.

— Nobody likes a show-off, Ryan.

Ryan rubbed the back of his neck.

— OK, Geoff Capes.

Liam rubbed his stomach.

— Let's go. I'm starving. You wanna eat at mine tonight?

Ryan bent his head back, rolling his neck across his shoulders, and sighed.

—I can't. It's Nathan's birthday meal. We're going out. I should get back.

Liam grimaced as he picked up his bike.

—Oooh. Lucky you.

Ryan puffed out his cheeks.

—Yeah. Lucky me.

The late-afternoon street is quiet as Ameliah walks alone past the terraced houses. A branded yellow paper shopping bag hangs from her right hand. She thinks about trying on clothes with Heather. Coming from behind the curtain in different tops like a show to a captive audience of one best friend and a few strangers in their underwear, Heather clapping her arrival each time with a huge grin on her face.

The others had looked shocked when she and Heather had arrived to meet them and they'd seen the bag Ameliah was holding. Each one of the girls asking a hundred questions and crowding round Ameliah like pigeons on a baguette.

She lifts the bag and peeks inside, reminding herself which top she bought. The navy blue material looks darker inside the bag.

A silver saloon car moves past her as she stands at the kerb and she pictures the man from the escalator. His stubbled face and dirty sand hair, like someone who used to be a skater.

She tries to give him a name, hoping it might jog her memory. Pete maybe, or Jack? Something strong and simple. No-nonsense.

Nothing seems to fit. But she has a funny feeling, like something isn't right. Like he shouldn't be here.

She fishes the new silver key from her pocket and feels the fresh jagged edge with her thumb. She thinks about the machine that cuts keys and looking up at it as a little girl, holding Dad's hand. Watching the man in the brown leather apron concentrating as he held the old key next to the new uncut one, matching it up perfectly before pressing it against the edge of the spinning wheel. The sound of metal being sanded away, like a dentist's drill on robot teeth.

She can hear voices as she closes the front door, muffled

through the wall. Nan's polite laugh intercut with the deeper weight of a man's voice, steady and definite.

Ameliah treads slowly towards the bottom of the stairs. As she reaches the oval mirror, the voices stop. She looks at her reflection, her eyes wide, looking towards the door.

She can hear her own breathing. The voices carry on and she creeps up the stairs, tiptoeing on the edges.

In her room she flops down on her back on to the bed, dropping the shopping bag on the floor by her feet. Light from the window splits the room in half. She listens to the voices downstairs, the man's deep tones followed by Nan's giggled response, and hopes he's not staying for dinner.

She sits up and reaches for the shopping bag. Standing in front of the mirror, she pulls her hoody over her head and drops it on to the bed. She looks at herself in just her jeans and white bra and thinks about Simone and the others with their make-up and earrings. The light from outside turns the skin on her slender shoulders a shade paler next to the dark of her thick curls.

She remembers doing dress-up with Dad back in the

old house. Drowning herself in one of his shirts underneath a smart waistcoat, his flat cap on her head, pretending to be an important explorer. Dad wearing his clothes backwards as her incompetent but lovable assistant.

Her arms crossed in front of her chest, she runs her fingertips down the skin of her upper arms, remembering the feel of the cotton shirt against her.

She reaches for her new top and pulls it over her head. The dark blue vest hangs perfectly on her and her eyes widen at how she immediately looks older. She lifts her hair up into a high bun at the back of her head and lowers her chin, staring into the mirror, attempting a pout, then laughing to herself.

The living-room door opens and Ameliah freezes. The mumbled voices become clearer, the man's deep laugh as Nan leads him out.

— Thank you again, Patricia, and I'll call you about next week?

— You're welcome, Richard. Yes, give me a ring.

— I look forward to it.

Ameliah doesn't move as she hears what sounds like a small kiss on the cheek and the heavy door pushed closed with a goodbye.

She lets her hair fall and stares through her open door at the top of the stairs. She can't hear any footsteps and imagines Nan standing there, lost in thought. She gets a flash of the man from the escalator, his thick scruffy hair, his eyes, and again she thinks of Mum. She remembers looking back towards the front door of the old house as she left for school, Mum waving to her like she was onstage in the school play.

Nan's footsteps head back towards the living room. Ameliah waits, expecting to be called, but only hears the living-room door pushed slowly closed. Her eyes fall on the dark hallway carpet. Who was the man on the escalator? And why did he make her think of Mum?

Ryan stared through the back-seat window at the lines of pink in the evening sky. He thought about smog and how unfair it was that the gases that made such pretty sunsets could be poisoning the earth. Nathan sat to Ryan's left, his face down in his new Game Boy. The leather fold-out armrest provided the barrier separating their halves of the car. In front of Ryan, Dad drummed the steering wheel along with the music as he drove. Sophia sat with her hands in her lap in the front passenger seat, smiling at the horizon.

— Can you see that sky, boys?

She craned her neck round towards the back seat. Nathan didn't look up. Ryan nodded a smile.

— It's like the apocalypse, he said.

Sophia's smile faded and she turned back to face the front.

— Maybe a bit dramatic, Ryan.

Dad laughed and pointed out of the window.

— Look! I can see four horsemen. This doesn't look good, guys. Nathan, we might have to skip the Harvester.

Nathan cursed under his breath, slapping the side of his Game Boy, then turned it off and dropped it between his thighs.

— What?

Dad raised his voice.

— I said, it looks like it's the end of the world, I'm afraid. We might have to skip the mixed grill!

Sophia turned down the music, leaving the end of Dad's sentence hanging in the air. Nathan cut Ryan a look.

— What's he talking about now?

Ryan shrugged.

— He's talking about your birthday causing the apocalypse.

He raised his eyebrows then turned back to stare out of the

window. Nathan raised a sarcastic thumb.

— Yeah. Good one, Michael. Mum, how much did Dad send?

Sophia shuffled in her seat uncomfortably.

— I'm not sure. It's not important now, let's just enjoy our meal.

She glanced towards Dad. Dad kept his eyes on the road.

Nathan turned to Ryan.

— My dad sent £130. Just for me. That's thirteen times ten.

Ryan stared out of the window and pictured a shoebox full of money. Large blue and white notes stacked up to the top. He thought about the excitement of getting the twenty-pound note inside his birthday card with the number 13 in thick red, and how many times he spent the money in his head that night.

It dawned on him that he knew almost nothing about Nathan's father. Not a name, a face or a job. All he knew was that he now lived in America and was, according to Nathan, very rich.

As the car curved round an island, Ryan noticed one old shoe hanging from the signpost by its laces.

He felt a dig in his leg and turned his head. Nathan stared straight at him.

— How much did you get on your birthday?

Sophia turned her head.

— Enough, Nathan. We're out for a nice meal to celebrate your birthday, don't spoil this.

Nathan looked at her and faked a smile. Sophia turned back to the front. Ryan looked at the back of Dad's head, the moulded plastic of his dark glasses tucked behind his ear.

They pulled into the car park right next to the large artificial yellow letters of the Harvester sign as the sunlight started to fade. Dad turned off the engine and clicked off the stereo. Sophia checked her hair in the small mirror of the fold-down sun visor. Nathan grabbed his Game Boy. Ryan tugged at his buttoned-up shirt collar and sighed as, all along the dual carriageway, streetlights flickered on.

Ameliah feels the thick play button depress under her fingertip. The crackle starts immediately. She turns the volume dial down, making the sound just audible, and stares at the stereo. Reaching into her pocket, she pulls out the shell and lays it on the bedside table next to the black mesh of the speaker. She stares at it as she backs away from the stereo towards the window. The familiar hiss she has heard every time she has played the tape now makes her smile.

She sits on the floor underneath the window in between a black bin bag full of clothes and a light brown suitcase turned on its side. She closes her eyes and lifts her chin, breathing in as though smelling her favourite meal. The mumbling voice speaks its underwater monologue over a bed of static and pops.

She looks to her right at the old poster she Blu-tacked on to the back of the closed bedroom door. The album artwork for *The Low End Theory*.

The green painted letters running down the back of the body made up of wavy red lines. She remembers staring at the same picture on Dad's CD as the album played on Sunday mornings.

She reaches for the old suitcase to her left that she dragged from the spare room earlier. Sliding the brass locks, she pops the clasps up and lifts the lid. Pieces of paper, letters and old photographs spill out on the floor.

Pressing the top of the bulging pile with her left hand, stopping the flow, she fishes inside with her right like she's choosing tickets in a raffle.

She feels the bumps of something stuck to paper and pulls it out on to her lap. The two stick-figure characters are drawn in rough blue and green crayon and have tubes of pasta stuck on to their limbs. Next to them more pasta tubes form the trunk of an out of proportion palm tree, its leaves the same size as the giant smiling heads next to it. Underneath them, against the pink sugar-paper background, the words Mum and Dad are written in writing that looks like somebody penned while riding a roller coaster. Ameliah reads her own name in the same warped letters in the bottom right corner.

She runs her fingertip along each of Dad's huge sausage fingers and remembers the picture on the fridge in the old house.

She remembers Mum pinning it on to the smooth white of the door with two magnets shaped like bottle tops and pulling her into a hug, kissing her temple. Mum always held hugs that little bit extra, just enough for you to know that she meant it.

Ameliah glances at her watch: 22:58 in black against the dark green background. It's late and she should probably sleep.

The old stereo speakers mumble words. Ameliah pricks her ears, hearing something new. The hiss covers the voice again. Ameliah gets up, dropping Mum and Dad on the floor next to her. The fountain of old papers gushes over the edge of the suitcase and on to the carpet as she moves to the stereo, presses stop then rewind. The tape squeaks as the spools spin in reverse. She clicks stop, grabs the pen from next to her lamp and presses play. The static starts and Ameliah leans in to try and discern the word. The muffled voice sounds like the cycle of a distant washing machine, the beat of low syllables on a slow cycle, then:

— I don't know, I was just trying to do something. I don't think he even realises how much he ruins things.

Ameliah stares at the chipped speaker nearest to her face.

Why hasn't she heard this before? Why can't she hear it all?

She reaches for the shoebox lid and stares at the words in dark ink. As the hissing static continues, she stares into space, tapping the cardboard lid with the end of her pen, the felt tip blotching blurred circles every time it connects.

— Who are you?

She shakes her head as she speaks, ready to laugh at herself, and then the speaker answers:

— Who, me?

The air inside the car was thick with the lingering argument from dinner. Sophia stared straight ahead as she drove. Ryan looked at the back of Dad's head in front of him, slumped heavy on his palm, trapping his hand against the glass. He imagined the view from high above them. The car's headlights becoming the blip of a homing device on the screen of some government agency keeping tabs on their whereabouts.

Behind Sophia, Nathan stared out of his window, grinding his teeth, his empty hands balling fists and releasing them over and over.

Ryan stared at the fold-down armrest. The dark brown felt looked like grizzly bear skin. He knew that there were people who were experts at saying something at times like this. People who had the kind of timing and judgement to completely lift the weight of a ruined celebration off everyone's shoulders. People like Mum.

Mum would've made some joke about still having corn in her

teeth that she was saving for supper or a comment about their waiter's walk that would make everyone smile, reluctantly at first, but once the dam had been broken with that first smirk, the atmosphere would lift and pretty soon everyone in the car would be laughing from their bellies.

Ryan thought of Mum's voice. The way words would just fall out of her mouth. Tumbling into the air, ready to make things better.

He thought about Eve. Her voice. How her accent had hit him in the park and how similar it was. He wondered whether Ireland only made perfect girls then remembered Tracey Cunnane from school and scrapped his theory.

He looked into the rear-view mirror. Sophia's eyes reflected the amber glow of an oncoming car then faded. He couldn't make out whether she was welling up or if it was just the light.

Sophia glanced in the mirror and their eyes met.

Ryan looked down. Sophia stared back at the road.

Ryan looked across at Nathan, the cause of the tension. His birthday meal ruined by his pushing the limits of what he could say to get a reaction. Dad switching to whisky and drinking quicker to avoid retaliating. Sophia torn between blowing her lid in a public place and trying to save the meal.

Ryan wondered whether Nathan felt bad. Whether he

behaved like he did in the moment and then felt guilty as he lay in bed, or if this was some kind of evil master plan to sabotage everything.

Whichever it was, it was clear to Ryan that Nathan was angry, and if he didn't think it would earn him a punch in the ribs and a headlock, he told himself he'd ask him why.

As the car turned into their street, Ryan was hit with a compulsion to rescue things. He racked his brain, trying to channel the essence of Mum. What would she say? Something funny. Something perfect. He felt his moment slipping as Sophia pulled the car up outside their house and switched off the engine. Dad groaned and slowly raised his head.

The car fell silent. Ryan took a deep breath, his mind drawing a complete blank, then, from nowhere:

— Phew. Anyone else really need a poo?

Everyone turned and stared at Ryan with an equal mix of confusion and disgust. Ryan cracked a weak smile and made a mental note to never try and be Mum again.

In his room, Ryan stared at the small red recording light on his boom box. The tiny teeth of the tape reels rotating like miniature hubcaps as he spoke.

— It was pretty bad, Mum. Dad wanted to say something, but

he just drank more and more instead. Nathan's such an idiot. How can someone be such an idiot? I had a burger. The car ride was proper moody. It's his fault. Then I had to go and open my mouth. I don't know, I was just trying to do something. I don't think he even realises how much he ruins things, you know?

He let out a long sigh and glanced at his radio alarm clock. The boom box hummed, still recording.

— Anyway, it's nearly eleven, Mum. I'm tired, I'm gonna go.

— Who are you?

Ryan felt his stomach drop. The voice of a girl. He looked over his shoulder. His room felt suddenly alive in the lamplight. He told himself to stop being stupid, that didn't just happen, but he couldn't let it go. He leaned in towards the speaker.

— Who, me?

The speakers crackled then there was just the hum of the tape. Ryan waited. Nothing. He sat up, scrunching up his face then shaking his head as he remembered Dad saying the first sign of madness was hearing voices. He puffed out his cheeks and pressed stop, watching the red light fade with the speakers' hum. He looked round the room again then lay down on his back, staring up at the ceiling, and told himself that he'd seen one too many science-fiction films.

Ameliah stares at the stereo. The tiny red light is on and she notices that the button next to play is pressed too. She must've accidentally pushed record and play together. She shivers and stabs the stop button with her finger. She feels the hairs on her arm stand up as the two buttons click off and the red light fades.

She looks round the room. The door is shut and the old suitcase under the window is partially buried by old papers and photos.

She thinks about what she told Simone and the others yesterday in the park, Dad's story about hearing a voice, and tells herself that her brain is playing games. She raps the top of her head with her knuckles like she's knocking on a door.

— I'm not stupid, you know. It's all just suggestion, I've seen David Blaine.

Her voice is eaten by the silence. She stares again at the stereo and feels her fingers reaching for the buttons. She is sure that didn't just happen, but her blood is bubbling with curiosity. She breathes in and, with her index and middle finger, presses record and play at the same time. As the plastic buttons depress, the red light comes on again. The speakers hum into life. Ameliah waits. Nothing but the hum. She leans closer.

— Hello? Is anyone there?

Her eyes drift across the room to the mirror on the back of the wardrobe door. She looks at herself, the dark rings under her eyes, leaning into the old stereo like an elderly woman trying to hear the news, and smiles as she speaks.

— What the hell are you doing?

Her reflection shakes its head and she presses stop. The hum dies and she lies back on to her bed, staring up at the ceiling. She feels her head sink into the pillow and her hair as she sighs and tells herself that she probably needs a hobby.

CHAPTER 4

Ryan stared at the doorbell then at the letter box. It was still early and he knew that the doorbell might wake Liam's dad, but that quietly knocking the letter box had left him standing on the doorstep for ages before.

He thought about the voice on the tape last night, picturing himself telling Liam, and Liam's big face curling into a smile as he laughed at him. He hadn't heard anything. Nothing real anyway.

Shaking his head, he looked up at the house and wished there was a better way to let Liam know he was here but, as Liam's room was at the back and the street was terraced houses all along, there really wasn't much he could do besides scaling the drainpipe, climbing over the roof and abseiling down to Liam's window.

He psyched himself up to press the bell quickly, one short blast that Liam would hear but wouldn't wake his dad.

Breathing out a long sigh, he raised his finger just as the front door opened and Jason stepped out.

Ryan stared up at Liam's older brother. Jason was nineteen and had the face of a man on top of his giant muscular body. His large T-shirt clung to broad shoulders, beanie hat pulled down over his shaved head. He smiled at Ryan.

— Good timing, littlun.

Jason's voice sounded like the man who speaks over film trailers, gravelly and strong, and fitted his body perfectly. He pulled his paint-splattered rucksack on to his shoulders as he passed Ryan on his way to the front gate. Ryan nodded a nervous smile. Jason was pretty much cool in a can. He worked in a factory that made car parts, and ran the under-sixteens football team at the working men's club on a Saturday, and always called Ryan 'littlun'. Even though it wasn't the most complimentary nickname, Ryan was still glad he'd been given it.

Jason slid his headphones over his ears and pointed with his thumb.

— He's upstairs trying to rap.

Ryan smiled and rolled his eyes.

— Thanks, Jayce. What you listening to?

Jason didn't hear as he headed out of the gate, on his way to make machines.

Ryan eased the door shut and tiptoed along the dark hallway towards the stairs. The top half of the walls had raised floral wallpaper, separated from the deep green of the painted bottom half by a thin strip of varnished wood.

Liam's house always smelled like it had just been hoovered as his mum was obsessed with Shake n' Vac. Ryan breathed in the mountain-fresh fragrance as he climbed the stairs. At the top, he stared at the door to Liam's parents' room down the landing. Halfway along, the bathroom door was open and light from the window cut a strip on to the dark floor like a warning barrier. Ryan lifted his weight up on to his toes and crept round the banister to the right.

As he passed Mary's room, he heard the sound of strummed guitar chords from inside. He stared at the poster on her door. The baby swimming underwater next to the word Nevermind. The strumming guitar turned horrible then stopped and he heard what sounded like two giggling voices from inside.

He quickly moved away, knocking lightly on Liam's bedroom door next to a hole roughly the size of a fist. The door stayed shut. Ryan pressed his ear to the painted wood, trying to hear sounds of life, just as Liam, wearing an emerald green dressing gown, pulled it open. Ryan fell forward, saving himself with his foot.

— Jesus! L—

— Sshhhhhhh.

Liam grabbed Ryan by the shoulder, looking past him into the hall, and pulled him into the room. Closing the door, he pushed Ryan up against it, pressing his thick finger against his closed lips.

— Quiet, man!

He broke into a smile and let Ryan go, walking over to his unmade single bed and sitting down.

— They'll hear you.

Ryan straightened his jumper and scanned the room. The balding blue carpet was covered in strewn clothes and magazines. On the left next to the window, a small fish tank sat on top of a cheap white desk. Sun shone through the water and glass, rippling light on Liam's legs as he sat.

Above Liam's pillow, a large poster showed a man in a kilt looking angry, holding a sword, above the word Highlander. To the right, the flesh-coloured plaster of the unpainted wall opposite the window was covered in attempts at graffiti letters and tags, a huge wonky purple letter 'L' the centrepiece.

Ryan slumped on to an old red beanbag on the floor near the door.

Liam's face looked excited.

— Ask me who?

Ryan looked at him.

— What?

— Ask me who'll hear.

Ryan shrugged his shoulders.

— What are you talking about, man? I was quiet. I tiptoed up the stairs. I stepped over the creaky bit on the landing—

— No. I mean in there.

Liam pointed to the wall behind Ryan's head, his eyes dancing. Ryan stared at him.

— Mary?

Liam shook his head, his smile widening.

— She's here.

He whispered the words, covering his mouth with his left hand, jabbing a point at the wall with his right.

— Your girl. Eve. She stopped the night.

Ryan felt his stomach flip over like a fish on the pavement. His eyes widened.

— *What?!*

Liam bit his bottom lip.

— She stopped the night. I didn't even know she was here till I came up to bed and heard them talking.

Ryan sat up and stared at the wall. He tried to imagine Eve in the next room, sitting with Mary on her bed, listening to Nirvana.

— Are you serious?! Don't mess me around, Liam.

— I'm not messing you around. She's in there now. How about that for mission accomplished?

Ryan stood up and moved to the wall, leaning in until his ear touched the cool smooth wallpaper.

— I can't hear anything.

— Here.

Liam held out an empty pint glass.

— Use this.

Ryan took the glass and placed it against the wall, pressing his ear to the bottom.

— I can hear the sea.

Liam shook his head.

— Give it a sec. You have to concentrate. It's like tuning in. Close your eyes.

Ryan closed his eyes and concentrated. He thought he could make out the murmur of voices. He saw Eve's face in his mind. Her dark hair framing her face. Her green eyes staring straight at him. He lowered the glass, smiling. Just knowing she was the width of a wall away felt amazing.

— So what are you going to do?

Liam stared straight at him. Ryan narrowed his eyes.

— What do you mean?

— I mean what are you going to do? You have to do something, right? This is some kind of sign. It has to be.

Ryan moved over to the bed. Liam shuffled along, making room for him to sit down.

— What do you expect me to do? Knock on the door and invite myself in? Hey, ladies, what you listening to? Nirvana? Cool, yeah, I play a bit of guitar myself and blah blah blah blah blah. I'm not gonna do anything.

Liam frowned.

— Ryan. She's right next door. This is too much of a coincidence. Now grow some balls and go lay it down.

Ryan felt butterflies in his stomach.

— Shut up, man.

— I'm serious. She's there, man, on a plate, I mean she's probably still in her pyjamas and everything. I wonder what pyjamas she's got? I bet they're really skimpy and—

— Shut up! I can't think.

Ryan stared across at the fish tank. Lines of sunlight cutting through into the room.

— You said she stopped the night?

— Yeah.

— OK, so her and Mary must be pretty close already.

— I guess so.

— Right, so there's no rush. There's no need to mess things up. We can just take our time and figure it out.

Liam shook his head.

— You may as well have a beak and white feathers.

Ryan looked at him, confused. Liam bent his arms, pushing his hands into his armpits.

— Why don't you fly a bit, Mr Chicken?

He flapped his pretend wings. Ryan shook his head.

— Chickens don't fly, you idiot.

Liam's face dropped.

— But they've got wings.

Ryan smiled.

— So have ostriches, and penguins. Have they had breakfast?

— Not even a little bit?

— No, trust me. They just run around and lay eggs, now have they had breakfast?

— Erm, I don't think so. They weren't awake when I got up and I haven't heard them leave the room.

Ryan's face lit up.

— Perfect. OK, so sooner or later they'll have to eat. They'll go downstairs for food and that's when we stroll through on our way out and say hi, real cool like.

Liam leaned forward.

— OK, good, then what?

— Then what what?

— Then what do we do?

Ryan shrugged.

— Then we leave.

Liam scrunched up his face.

— That's it. We say hi and then leave?

Ryan stood up and started to pace.

— Yep. It'll be perfect. She'll know who I am, I'll hear her voice again, no pressure, just sowing the seed.

He kneeled down in front of the fish tank. A speckled orange and white fish stared out at him with one eye.

Liam stood up.

— What seed?

Ryan tapped the glass with his fingertip. The fish darted away.

— It doesn't matter. Just get dressed man, we have to be ready.

Ameliah stares at the pyramid of black bags. The top bag is level with her head as she stands barefoot in her grey jogging bottoms and white vest on the sky-blue spare room carpet. The house is quiet, Nan already gone to work.

She smiles to herself, thinking about the voice on the tape and how she'd woken up and tried again. Pressing the two buttons, watching the red light and waiting to hear. How all she'd heard was the hum of the tape and how she'd told herself that she needed something to occupy an overactive imagination. She hadn't heard anything. Nothing real anyway.

Something catches the light, wedged between the bags and the tower of boxes to her right. She leans in and moves the black plastic, feeling the soft clothes inside the bag, and sees the head of a guitar, the silver metal tuning pegs against the light tan of the wood. She wraps her finger around it and pulls slowly but strongly. The neck moves slightly, but the body is firmly wedged in.

She has a flashing image of Mum onstage wearing face paint, screaming into a mic, thrashing her guitar.

She uses her shoulder to push the bags on her left away, making space, and pulls again. The neck of the guitar is now visible, the copper-coloured strings against the dark varnish of the fret. She gives a last tug and falls backwards as the guitar comes free, landing on her back with it on top of her like it's pinning her for a three count.

She laughs to herself, holding the belly of the guitar in her hands. It feels lighter that she thought it would.

She sits up and turns it round, resting the bottom on the carpet. The light wood of the body looks old but not worn. She counts five strings and realises she has no idea if that's enough or too little. She remembers Mum playing, sitting in her room on Sunday nights after the bath, wrapped in a towel, hair still wet, looking up at her as she played with closed eyes. She remembers feeling like she'd been let in on a secret. Mum's eyes opening as she finished her song, her smiling, but for some reason the image has no sound.

Looking over her shoulder, Ameliah sits up straight, laying the guitar across her lap ready to play. Her left hand cradles the neck, her fingertips pressing the strings, feeling the hard ridges of the metal digging in near her nails. Her right hand hangs over the body, pretending to hold a plectrum ready to strum. She looks down, her tongue between her teeth in concentration, and brushes the strings firmly.

The ugly gang of notes growls out and she feels the vibration against her stomach. She smiles with the satisfaction of making sound. Biting her bottom lip, she strums again, this time louder. She doesn't know whether it's a chord or not but carries on strumming, forcing a rhythm with her right hand.

Her head starts to nod and her mouth opens.

— Yeah yeah. Guitaaaaaaar. I can't play iiiiit.

The fingertips of her left hand give up, stinging from the pressure, and she stops. The notes die away and the room falls quiet.

Get out of the way, Liam!

Mary's voice cut through the TV sounds and Ryan imagined her face on the other side of the partition wall. He looked at Liam, the only one visible to him. Liam shrugged.

— Chill out, sis. We're just getting a drink. Who's your friend?

Ryan felt to run. He took a step backwards towards the door. He figured he could get along the hall and out of the front door before Liam got anywhere near him but, as he heard her voice, his feet wouldn't move.

— I'm Eve.

— Hi, Eve. I'm Liam.

— So you're the big little brother?

Liam smiled a cocky smile and rolled his shoulders like he was warming up to lift weights.

— Yep. That's me. So you're Irish, I mean proper Irish?

He gave a cheesy chat-show smile, not noticing Ryan stabbing a finger at the kitchen, trying to get his attention.

— Liam. Get out of the way of the telly right now or I swear to God I'm gonna scratch your face.

Mary's voice was sharp. Liam's face changed and he stepped to the side.

— OK, OK, easy, sis. There you go. What you watching anyway? *Dirty Dancing*? Again? You don't get tired of it, do you? She's seen it more than twenty times, Eve, I'm not kidding.

Ryan felt himself starting to sweat as he watched. His fingers curled into fists by his side, knowing that any second Liam was going to drag him into the conversation. Then she spoke again.

— Me too. I know it's silly, but when he lifts her up, ah, I love that bit.

Her voice was calm, like she'd just woken up happily from a nap. Ryan watched Liam nodding in response and it dawned on him that his friend wasn't actually that bad at talking to girls and this was actually going pretty well. He felt his fingers relaxing as a woman with blond hair shouted at Patrick Swayze on the screen.

— So whereabouts in Ireland are you from?

Liam carried on his small talk, seemingly enjoying how it was going.

— What? Shut up, Liam. Leave her alone, we're watching the film. What do you want?

— Nothing. Keep it down, will ya, you'll wake Dad up. Ryan's here, look. Come say hello, Ryan.

He beckoned Ryan over like a little kid. Ryan stepped slowly towards his friend like he was walking on to a stage.

He told himself not to stare at her as he stood next to Liam, gazing straight ahead into the mirror on the wall behind the sofa.

He felt both girls looking at him as he noticed how big Liam seemed next to him.

— Hi, Ryan.

Mary smiled. Ryan nodded shyly, feeling the inside of his trainers with his toes.

— Hi, Mary. Sorry to spoil your film. I told him we should just get a drink.

Liam frowned.

— What?

— It's all right. I've learned to live with Mr Subtle.

She rolled her eyes in Liam's direction. Liam looked at her then at Ryan then back to her again. Ryan's eyes were on Mary, but he could feel Eve looking at him.

— You were in the park the other day.

Her voice seemed to pour into his ears and he could feel it running down the back of his neck. She remembered him. He could feel his blood getting warm. She remembered him.

— Yeah. Ryan likes Irish girls.

Ryan felt his body go numb. He looked at Liam.

— He loves 'em. Where did you say you were from?

Mary and Eve looked at each other, their eyes narrow. Mary looked at Ryan.

— She didn't. So you like Irish girls, Ryan?

Ryan felt their eyes burning into him.

— No. I mean, yeah. I don't know what he's talking about. What are you talking about, Liam?

He shrugged up at his best friend in desperation. Liam saw him struggling.

— I mean his mum was Irish. Ryan's mum was Irish. She's dead now.

The room seemed to stop. Nobody spoke. Ryan felt like he was going to melt into the carpet. He imagined himself slowly shrinking away into a puddle like the bad guy from *Who Framed Roger Rabbit*, his best friend, his sister and the most beautiful girl he'd ever seen powerless to help him.

Liam's mouth moved, like his tongue was fishing for words in the air in front of him. Mary forced a smile through pursed lips. Ryan looked at Eve, her green eyes staring straight into him. He felt his lungs pressing against the inside of his chest as he breathed in then ran out of the room.

Ameliah tilts the plastic carton to vertical, finishing the last of the milk. She can feel the cold from inside the open fridge on her stomach through her vest. She wipes her milk moustache away with the back of her hand and thinks about cowboys in saloons swigging moonshine and spitting tobacco.

The tiles of the kitchen floor are warm against the soles of her feet. She bends down to look into the fridge, her eyes scanning the bulging shelves of meats and salad stuff. She reaches in and pulls out a plate of leftover pizza, the thick triangles pointing over the edge.

She scratches the back of her neck and smiles, looking down at herself.

— I'm a slob.

She hears a dog barking a few gardens away.

— Slobby slob.

She arches her back, sticking out her stomach, trying to give herself a belly, then gives up, taking a big bite from a slice of pizza as she walks out of the kitchen.

In the living room she sits on the floor with her back against the sofa, her thumb pressing a steady beat on the remote control, flicking through channels. The jumping snippets of conversation from different programmes sound like they're trying to make a sentence.

She thinks about the tape. The blurred sound of the young voice. On the TV screen a round-faced man holds up a large fish in two hands, his face full of pride. Ameliah stares at the fish. The fish stares back, its big round glossy eye looking into her. She looks at its wide mouth, gaping to breathe.

— What does it mean, Mr Fish? Eh?

The man wobbles in his boat as the fish twists its body, trying to get away. He raises his eyebrows, his forehead glistening with sweat.

— Wow, you can feel the power in him. Let's get him back in the water, shall we?

Ameliah takes another bite of pizza, pointing the doughy crust in her hand at the screen.

— Yeah. You put him back before he slaps your face. Go on, Mr Fish, slap his face.

The street was quiet as Ryan walked alone past the terraced houses. He stared at his shadow, stretching out away from him, like Flat Stanley. He remembered Mum reading him the story on the sofa, his head on her lap, looking up at her as she spoke. They talked about folding themselves up to fit inside letters and where they'd send them to.

He had said Timbuktu because he liked the sound of the word. Mum said Galway where her parents lived so she could surprise them.

She had explained to him that nothing in the world was actually truly flat. That even a piece of paper had a depth that meant it was three-dimensional. Ryan remembered quizzing her with a list of things he thought of as flat and her smiling and shaking her head each time. Even clingfilm.

A woman on a bicycle passed him on the road in the other direction and Ryan thought about Eve, staring at him after Liam opened his big mouth. What did she think? Who just runs out of a room?

He shook his head as he approached his house, reaching into his pocket, and realised he didn't have his key. He'd left that morning without it, not expecting to be back until later when Dad and Sophia would be home.

He stood at the gate and stared at the front window. The net curtains stopped anyone seeing in, Sophia's choice. When Ryan had argued that they meant nobody could see out either, which was surely the whole point of a window, she had just smiled at him like he was a baby getting the alphabet wrong.

He thought about people walking past the house every day. Strangers who had no idea about the changes that had happened on the inside. The house was a number, 184, just like any other on the street, and Ryan wondered how many other families on the street had lost a member.

He looked up to the smaller bedroom window and saw Nathan staring down at him, his arms folded like some kind of prison guard from an old film.

An imposter in his house, acting like he owned it. He stared back up at Nathan, trying to seem bigger than he was.

Nathan smiled an evil smile and held up something, shaking it in his hand. Ryan knew it was his key even though he couldn't fully make it out from this distance. Nathan pulled a mock surprised face, bringing his free hand to his chest.

Ryan stared up, knowing what came next; he would plead, Nathan would leave him locked out, maybe dangle the key through the letter box, tempting him, he'd go to grab it and Nathan would pull it away, laughing, and then it would start over again.

Nathan began to laugh, the space between them muting his voice, making him look like a rubbish mime artist. Ryan lifted his hand in front of his face and flicked two fingers. Nathan's face dropped, his laughter turning at first to confusion then quickly to anger. He started shouting something on mute, waving his hands angrily, as Ryan turned and walked away from the house, back the way he had come.

The sound of the front door stirs Ameliah awake. On the TV a woman with a pointy face examines an old vase while a fat lady sits watching her with a smile.

The last bit of pizza crust falls off Ameliah's chest on to the floor as she sits up. She quickly picks up any large crumbs and drops them on to the plate, searching for the remote control behind her.

— Am!

Nan's voice calls from the hall. Ameliah hears her flicking through post.

— Ameliah!

Nan walks into the room dressed in a smart white blouse and dark trousers. Her thick frame looks sturdy rather than plump.

— Oh, there you are, love. You OK?

She tears open a letter and starts to read. Ameliah rubs her eyes with her knuckles.

— Yeah. Yeah, I'm fine. Good day?

Nan stares at the letter.

— Oh, you know. Same same. We've had some bigwigs from head office in so everyone's on their best behaviour.

— You look smart.

Nan lowers the letter and glances down at herself. She smacks her lips.

— Thank you, love. I scrub up OK, don't I?

Ameliah smiles.

— Yeah.

The fat woman on the TV loses her smile as the woman with the pointy face hands her back her vase.

— How about you? You get in the spare room?

Ameliah wipes her mouth with the back of her hand, feeling the dribble from her unplanned nap.

— Yeah. A little bit. I found Mum's guitar.

Nan fishes around in her bag.

— Pardon, love?

— Mum's guitar. I found it. Buried in with the bags.

Nan pulls out a DVD.

— Oh yeah, that's lovely.

Ameliah's eyes narrow.

— I was thinking maybe I could learn.

Nan smiles, blowing out her cheeks. She looks at Mum's photograph on top of the TV.

— OK, love, whatever you like. It's pretty tough-going though.

— What?

— I'm just saying, it's hard work, that's all. Your fingers get all hard and it takes hours to even master the basics.

Ameliah stares at Nan.

— Yeah, well, I think I could do it. I mean maybe I won't get as good as Mum, but—

— Do what you like, love. Have you eaten? I'll make a start on some food.

Ameliah watches Nan thinking about more than one thing at once, her face wrestling with hiding what she's feeling.

— What's wrong, Nan?

Nan puffs out her cheeks.

— Nothing, love. Guitar. Great.

She holds up the DVD in her hands.

— *True Grit.* I think he won an Oscar for this one.

Ameliah looks at the wobbling case, at Nan's hands trying not to shake.

— What do you fancy for dinner? I've got some work bits to do, but we'll watch it tonight, yeah?

Nan glances at the photograph on top of the TV then looks at her, forcing a smile. Ameliah shrugs and nods.

— Cool.

Ryan pressed stop on tape deck two, hearing Nathan come out of his room. The red recording light faded as he sat up, ready for Nathan to barge in. He told himself that that proved it – he'd imagined the voice. The part of his brain that generated ideas must be underused or something. He had girls on the brain, that was it. More specifically, one girl. One girl who probably now thought he was a total weirdo for running off.

He heard Nathan's footsteps head across the landing and breathed out as the bathroom door opened.

Ryan pressed eject and pulled out the tape. He tapped the dark plastic with the side of his thumb and thought about how many times he'd recorded his voice on to it. He wasn't sure how many exactly, but he knew it must be a lot of words.

He wondered what happened to the words from before each time he recorded new ones. Was it like a field that gets ploughed, with the old words getting turned over and new ones lying on top? Where did they go?

Was it like those drawing toys you got in party bags where you pulled the slide out and it wiped away your picture?

He stared at the dark rolls of tape inside the plastic as the bathroom door locked.

Surely the old words must still be there. Like layers. Like each time he recorded he was painting a new layer on top of the ones before, only the tape never got any thicker.

He felt his head starting to hurt and told himself to stop. There were some things that he would never understand; like Mum used to say, people who need to understand everything are the worst company.

He picked up the empty cassette box and slid the tape inside, then opened the drawer of his bedside table and dropped the tape in.

Rolling on to his back, he stared up at the ceiling. He could hear the sound of Nathan in the shower through the wall. Ryan narrowed his eyes and squeezed his lips together, trying to mentally make the shower water run cold.

I remember lying in bed; it's late but I'm not asleep. I don't know why. You're downstairs — I can hear the mumble of the TV. Mum is out with friends. My bedroom door is open and I'm thinking about trying to sneak downstairs and ask to stay up with you, maybe watch the end of whatever film you're watching like you sometimes let me do, then the bell goes.

I know it's too late for visitors and I think that Mum must've forgotten her key and I hear you going to the front door, your footsteps are angry because you know she might have woken me up, and I want to see so I sneak to the top of the stairs and I can feel the cold air from the open front door and I see the back of you, slumped against the door frame, and the young policewoman touches your shoulder and looks at her partner, and he doesn't know where to look, and the light from outside is bouncing off their uniforms and the policewoman nods and they lead you inside and I feel like I'm stuck to the floor.

I want to call down and ask what's happened, but my voice isn't there. I can feel the heat of my breath in

my throat, but I can't make any sound. I hear the rustle of their police jackets, but their shoes don't make any noise as they walk you into the living room. Your hand is across your face and I know it's bad and I don't know what to do.

It's funny how the really, really good stuff and the really bad stuff feel like a film, you know? When your mind plays it back and you try to see, it feels like you're watching a screen, only the actors are you and the people you know, and the film just keeps on going.

I remember hearing people talking, at the funeral, I don't know who it was, I just remember them saying, 'They had to cut her out.' The car was so smashed up they had to cut away the metal to get to her. Weird as it sounds, I pictured those little trees, you know, the really small ones they have in Japan and people look after them with little scissors and delicately snip and cut, trimming the leaves.

Imagine if that was your job? To cut people out of cars.

They said she died instantly, that when she swerved and the bus hit her, there wouldn't even have been time to think, but I don't believe that.

The brain is fast. Mum always said that. She said somebody could think a hundred things in a second if they had to.

You remember me asking you that? What she thought, in that last second?

You said she thought about me. You sat on my bed and you said that she thought about me and that she smiled. And I cried till I couldn't breathe.

CHAPTER 5

— Am. Am. *Ameeeliaaaaaaaah!*

The voice lifts Ameliah's eyelids. She feels her head heavy on her pillow. Her legs curl up towards her chest underneath the duvet, trying to climb back into sleep.

— Wakey-wakey.

Ameliah smiles as she recognises Heather's voice and feels the weight of her best friend on the end of the bed. She pulls the duvet over her shoulders up to her ears.

— What time is it?

— It's nearly half nine. What were you dreaming about, was it that boy?

— What? What boy?

— From the park. The other day, he was nice, so what happened?

Ameliah feels her eyes starting to focus.

— What happened when?

— In your dream, was he naked?

Ameliah laughs.

— Shut up, Heather. I didn't dream anything.

Heather stands up and peels off her thin sky blue hoody. Her dark straight hair is tied up in a ponytail.

— OK, whatever you say. I saw you look at him though. You know, you're allowed to dream. Last night I dreamed that me and Ricky Moran were in this big swimming pool full of this weird pink water, bit like a lava lamp, both of us completely naked, you know he had a massive—

— OK, I get it. Did Nan let you in?

— Yeah, with that man.

Ameliah looks at Heather.

— What man?

Heather pouts into the wardrobe mirror, feeling her cheek with her fingertips.

— The man downstairs.

Ameliah sits up.

— What man downstairs, Heather?

— I don't know, he's a man. He's pretty handsome actually. For an older guy, I mean.

— Is it Richard?

Ameliah leans forward. Heather turns to her.

— Who's Richard?

— Heather, did he say his name was Richard?

— I don't know. I didn't really speak to him. I got here and he was standing on the step, about to knock on the door.

— What did he look like?

Ameliah watches Heather think.

— He didn't look like a Richard.

— What does that even mean?

— It means he didn't look like a Richard. Richard is, I don't know, it's not right, he looked more like a Jack or a Jake or a Carlos.

— Carlos?

— I dunno. Something strong. And moody. What do you care anyway?

Ameliah leans against the wall behind her pillows.

— I don't. It probably is Richard. I think he's trying to get with my nan.

Heather looks surprised.

— I don't think so, I mean no disrespect to your nan, but this guy is a lot younger than her.

Heather sits down on the bed. Ameliah moves her legs across to give her more room. Heather smiles cheekily.

— Why don't we go down and check him out? Sweat him out a bit?

— Sweat him out?

— Yeah, you know, ask him some personal questions, watch him squirm. It'll be fun.

Ameliah smiles at her.

— You're such a bitch.

Heather shrugs.

— I'm just saying. Between us we could probably suss him out. I mean if he's after your nan and he's that much younger than her, there must be something dodgy about him, no?

Ameliah pictures Nan, hypnotised into a trance. Her eyes are glazed as she hands a cheque over to a greasy younger man in a dark green suit, smiling a smile with too many teeth.

She kicks Heather from under the duvet.

— Let's do it.

Ryan squeezed a thick line of brown sauce on to his scrambled eggs. He reached the edge and doubled back, making a 'V'. He thought about writing SOS. A burnt brown call for help on an eggy beach. Across the table from him Sophia shook her head.

— Have you seen what that stuff does to an old 2p coin?

To his right Nathan rolled his eyes as he cut into a thick sausage. To his left Dad sipped his tea, his elbows on the table, holding his mug in both hands. Ryan looked back at Sophia. He wondered how old he would say she was if he didn't already know.

It struck him that she looked a little bit like Maid Marian from the Robin Hood film with Kevin Costner. He didn't know the actress's name.

— Does that not bother you, Ryan?

She opened both hands as she asked. Ryan thought about the Sheriff of Nottingham and looked at Nathan.

— Robin Hood.

Everyone looked at him, confused.

— I mean not really. If it cleans a 2p, then maybe it's cleaning my stomach.

Nathan went back to his sausage.

— Weirdo.

Ryan imagined jumping across the table, pinning Nathan down and pushing the rest of the sausage into his mouth.

Dad put down his mug.

— Now look, boys. This is what we've been talking about. Every time we sit down this happens. The other night was totally spoiled by you behaving like little children.

Nathan looked at Sophia then at Dad.

— He started it. He's a weirdo.

— Stop it, Nathan.

Sophia leaned forward and pointed a finger at him. She reached for Dad's hand and their fingers locked together. As they looked at each other, Ryan knew something was coming.

— Sophia—

Dad interrupted himself.

— *We* think that all of us need a little help to get along.

Ryan looked at Nathan. Nathan stared back. They both looked at Dad and Sophia.

— We had a talk and we've decided that what would be great for us all would be some time together. Out of the house.

Ryan felt his stomach drop. He looked at Nathan and for the first time ever he got the impression that they were both thinking exactly the same thing. As Dad's mouth opened to carry on, he imagined freezing time. Dad and Sophia suspended in motion, their faces fixed solid as he and Nathan stood up and walked out before they could deliver what was obviously going to be rubbish news.

— So we've looked around and booked us a trip.

Nathan frowned.

— What kind of trip? Where to?

Dad looked at Sophia. Sophia smiled, her voice excited.

— It's called Haven Holidays. They're apartment-style caravans right next to the sea, in Devon. Five days.

Ryan tried not to pull a face. He felt all the muscles in his neck tighten, straining to keep looking neutral. Nathan didn't make the same effort.

— What? No. I'm not going. Five days? Just the four of us? In some stupid caravan? No way!

Ryan agreed completely, but bit his tongue.

Dad shrugged his shoulders.

— Well, we thought you might not be keen, Nathan, so we had a back-up plan.

Ryan looked at Dad. Nathan looked at Sophia.

— Yeah? And what's that?

Dad smiled.

— To force you.

The pleasure in his voice was clear. Ryan watched Dad squeeze Sophia's hand and, even though he wasn't happy about the idea of the trip at all, he felt good for Dad getting his moment.

Nathan turned to Sophia in protest.

— Mum! You cannot be serious. Tell him he can't force me to do anything.

Sophia pursed her lips.

— I'm sorry, Nathan. We talked all about it. We think it'll be good for us. We just need you to make the effort. OK?

She looked at Ryan. Ryan felt his shoulders slump. Dad reached out and laid his hand on Ryan's arm.

— OK, mate?

Ryan felt his face wrinkling up as the words left his mouth.

— When?

Dad glanced at Sophia then looked at Ryan and Nathan.

— Tomorrow.

— This is bullshit!

Nathan threw down his fork and stood up. Sophia looked shocked.

— Nathan! You watch your mouth! Sit down!

— No. And if you think I'm gonna get in the car and drive with you to some stupid caravan, you must be crazy. Wait till I tell Dad!

He stormed out of the room, stomping up the stairs.

Ryan stared at his scrambled eggs. The brown sauce had soaked into the fluffy yellow.

Sophia sighed heavily.

— I told you. Didn't I?

143

Dad shook his head.

— Don't worry. He'll come round. He'll have to. Besides, Ryan'll help convince him, won't you, Ryan?

Ryan looked at Dad and wondered if he even remembered ever being thirteen.

Ameliah feels her fingers tingle as she stares at the man sitting next to Nan on the sofa. His stubbled chin and bird's-nest hair. He sits upright like someone who either takes care of their body or is on edge. His T-shirt is different, a royal blue now, but he's the man from the escalator in town. She still can't place him, but her gut tells her something is wrong. She feels Heather's arm brush hers as they both stand in front of the sofa like they're about to perform a dance routine. She looks at Nan, smiling too much, like a nurse about to give an injection.

— Where's Richard?

Her voice cuts out of her mouth, stabbing the air between them. Nan frowns.

— Excuse me?

— Richard. Where is he?

Ameliah can feel the man looking at her. Something about him is tense. Nan touches her hair, embarrassed.

— What has Richard got to do with anything? What do you know about Richard?

— I know this isn't him.

Ameliah feels powerful in her standing position. Nan shifts in her seat.

— I think you should remember your manners, young lady. This is Joe. He's an old friend of your dad's.

Ameliah feels the wind knocked out of her sails at the mention of Dad. She racks her brains trying to place the man in her memory. Who is he? Where has she seen him before? She can feel Heather shifting her weight between her feet, uncomfortable in the situation.

The man stands up. He's at least six feet tall, not big, but strong-looking. Like he could be quick if he wanted to be. His face is awkward, like he's trying really hard.

— Pleased to meet you, Ameliah.

Ameliah notices Nan's nervous face, waiting for her response. She stares at the man. His voice is deep but clear and holds the slight twang of an American accent. She gets a flash of the voice, shouting maybe, a long time ago.

Her eyes narrow, her stomach tight.

— Shake the man's hand, Ameliah. I'm sorry, Joe, I don't know what's wrong with her.

Joe turns to Nan. Ameliah thrusts her hand forward while he's not looking, shaking his hand quickly. His palm is dry next to hers and his grip feels deceptive, like he's holding back.

He looks at Ameliah and she pulls her hand from his, dropping it to her side, looking him up and down. She can feel Nan's eyes on her. Joe lowers his hand.

— You look like your mum.

Ameliah squirms inside her baggy T-shirt. She looks at his hands and notices he doesn't have a wedding ring. She feels Heather tugging on her pyjama bottoms. Joe forces a smile.

— How old are you now?

She is sure she knows his voice. Nan stands up. Ameliah chews her lip.

— She's thirteen going on thirty-three. I'll make tea. Would you like breakfast, Joe?

Joe turns to Nan.

— I would love to, Patricia, but I can't stop, I have work to do. I just wanted to drop by and leave you my contact details.

Ameliah watches Nan smile back at him and exaggerate a nod.

— Well, thanks very much for coming and feel free to pop in any time.

She glances at Ameliah.

— We're usually a lot more hospitable. Where did you say you were staying again?

— I just moved into a flat nearer town. I haven't even unpacked. It's a real mess.

Nan looks at Ameliah and Heather.

— Joe works at the university. He recently moved back from the States. He's, what did you say you did again sorry? My mind's like a sieve.

Ameliah watches Joe's mouth as he fakes a polite laugh.

— That's OK. It's a bit techy. I'm doing a research project, I just got my funding through. It's physics, sort of.

— So you're a professor then?

Ameliah cuts in and stares at Joe. Nan looks nervous. Joe stares back at Ameliah.

— Yes. I am.

— My dad was a professor. Is that how you knew him?

She watches Joe's throat as he swallows.

— Yes, I know he was, a good one too, and no, that's not how I knew him. I knew him before then.

— When?

Ameliah holds his stare. Joe eyes are serious, like he's weighing her up. Nan cuts in.

— Let me show you out, Joe. It was lovely to meet you.

She gestures towards the door. Ameliah grabs Heather's hand as Nan leads him out. Just as he steps out of the room, Joe looks back, straight at her. Ameliah stares back. Then he's gone.

— What the hell are you doing?

Heather struggles to whisper, slapping Ameliah's shoulder with the back of her hand.

— That was so rude!

Ameliah stares at the living-room door, hearing Nan thank Joe again and close the front door. She adjusts her feet, planting herself as Nan's footsteps head back.

— What on earth was that, young lady?

Nan rests her hand on her hip.

— Why the attitude?

Heather looks down nervously.

— Hello, Heather. How are you?

— I'm fine, thank you, Patricia.

— Well? I'm waiting, Ameliah.

Ameliah shrugs.

— Who is he?

Nan rolls her eyes.

— His name is Joe and he's an old friend of your father's.

— Really? Says who? Him?

— I've got no idea why you behaved like that, but if it was up to me, you'd be running down the street right now to give him an apology. He's perfectly nice. Look, he gave me his address and his number, in case we need it.

She holds up a folded piece of torn white paper. Ameliah can see the edge of letters in black ink. She blows air out of her mouth.

— Need it for what? What about Richard?

— What the hell has Richard got to do with this?

— I don't know, you tell me.

Nan's eyes close as she sighs.

— I can't deal with you when you're like this. I'm sorry, Heather, you'll have to excuse me, I'm going for a lie-down. There's food in the fridge. Make sure to leave me a note if you go out.

Heather nods politely as Nan walks out of the room and starts upstairs. Ameliah bites her teeth together.

— Can you believe her?

Heather turns to her.

— You were a bit harsh, Am.

Ameliah frowns.

Heather shrugs.

— I told you though, didn't I? He definitely didn't look like a Richard.

Ryan moved over to the window and stared down into the narrow back garden. Nathan sat at the top end, his head down, scratching a line into the ground with a broken stick. A battered white leather football sat next to him on the thin grass.

Ryan glanced right then left. The back gardens of all the

houses in the street were like stamped copies of each other with their small rectangle of slabs at the bottom near the house and then patchy grass up to the back fence. He imagined that from above they'd look like the spines of books on a shelf.

At the top of the garden, beyond the fence, the gardens of the next street reached up to the backs of those houses. A mirror image of this side.

Ryan watched Nathan. He could tell he was still fuming. It looked like his mouth was moving as he dragged the stick back and forth and Ryan imagined him mumbling swear words like Muttley from *Wacky Races*.

He remembered Dad's and Sophia's faces when they talked about the holiday. The way they'd continuously glanced at each other nervously as they spoke. He knew they were both finding it hard and Ryan felt himself torn between feeling sorry for them, and also pleased that it wasn't working out.

He thought about Mum. How this had been her house, her choices. How, if he was to get a forensic team to dust for prints, Mum's finger tips would be all over the place. Her footprints in the carpet. Tiny signature spirals on the light switches and the forks. She walked differently to Sophia. When he lay in bed and heard feet coming up the stairs, Sophia's steps were different. Lighter somehow. Like she wasn't sure.

He stared through the window. Nathan now seemed to be trying to stab the ball with the stick, his hand bouncing off with each strike.

Ryan thought about Nathan's dad, thousands of miles away somewhere in America. He turned to his bed, staring at his boom box sitting on the bedside table, and imagined Mum's voice.

Heather sits on the floor, holding the guitar like a curious chimpanzee, turning it round, staring into the belly.

— You should learn, Am.

— Yeah, maybe. Not now.

Heather looks up at Ameliah sitting on her bed.

— Was she good, your mum?

Ameliah sticks out her bottom lip, her knees up by her chest.

— Yeah. She was. I know his face.

— That's so cool.

Heather lays the guitar across her folded legs and mimes playing, shaking her head from side to side.

— You should so learn.

She stares up at Ameliah.

— Seriously. Like her – it's probably in your genes or whatever.

Ameliah tries to picture Mum, sitting where Heather sits now, the guitar in her lap, playing with a smile.

She stares out of the window. Heather shrugs and continues to mime playing.

— I know I've seen him before.

Heather stops miming.

— Who? Richard?

— Joe.

Heather lays the guitar on the floor next to her.

— Yeah, from the escalator.

Ameliah shakes her head.

— No, I mean before, in the past. I just can't remember where. I think I remember him shouting.

— Shouting? He came to say hello, Am. If he knew your dad, it makes sense. He didn't seem dodgy to me.

Ameliah swings her legs over the edge of the bed. Her eyes are drawn to the old stereo.

— Something's not right. I can't place him, but I just know it's not a good memory.

Heather sits on the bed next to her.

— How do you know that?

— I just know, all right? You know actually I can't believe her, carrying on with some guy, and then inviting some other random guy in, just cos he says he knew my dad.

Heather smiles.

— Am, your nan said he just moved back here. If he's just moved back here and he knew your dad, then it makes sense to come, right? Pay respects and stuff?

— Yeah, if he did actually know him.

Ameliah stares at Heather. Heather looks back, lifting her eyebrows.

— You think maybe you just don't want to think about your dad?

— But why now? Six months after he dies?

Heather looks at her. Ameliah can feel the inside of her throat tightening.

— Why does he show up now? Just when I start going through stuff. Just when I find the tape?

She hears the words coming out of her mouth without thinking. Heather looks confused.

— What tape?

Ameliah reaches down the side of her bed and grabs

the shoebox lid. She holds it up to show Heather. Heather reads the words.

— *Since he showed up, it's different now, I miss you, Eve.* What does that mean?

— You see?

— See what, Am?

Heather is still lost.

— It was on the tape. A voice said those words and now he just turns up?

— What? What voice? What tape?

Ameliah reaches out to the stereo and presses eject, pulling out the old cassette and holding it up like evidence.

— This one. Weird, no?

Heather looks at the tape then back at Ameliah.

— Whose voice?

— I don't know, does it matter? Since he showed up, it says, and then some guy rocks up saying he knew my dad? Why now?

Heather shuffles closer to her.

— Am, are you OK?

Ameliah frowns.

— Don't do that, Heather. Don't look at me like I'm crazy.

155

— I'm not.

— Yes you are.

— Am, it's the summer holidays. If he works at the uni, he has the same calendar as us. He must've been working till they broke up and now he's moved back to get ready in time for September. Yeah?

Ameliah considers mentioning the other night. Speaking to the voice through the stereo – the way it seemed to hear her and respond. That didn't happen though. That wasn't real.

She feels a switch flick in her head. The same switch that lets her go into autopilot whenever she gets stuck talking to someone who has to share their condolences or say they're sorry for her loss. She looks at Heather's open face, miles away from knowing what it feels like, but full of love. She tells herself it isn't Heather's fault.

Heather moves even closer to her so their knees are touching.

She lays her hand on Ameliah's thigh with the same pressure as all the other hands from the last three years since Mum, then again for Dad. Hands that want to show concern and love and strength. Hands that feel like they could just as easily belong to mannequins.

— Yeah. You're right. Sorry.

Heather smiles. She looks down at the shoebox lid. Ameliah watches her wait for the air to feel calm enough to carry on then her face changes.

— It said your mum's name?

— Yeah.

— That is pretty weird, I mean timing wise, right?

Ameliah feels her lungs fill with air.

— Yeah.

Heather furrows her brow.

— What do we do?

Ameliah jumps up and bounces over to the window. She lifts up the lid of the old suitcase and starts digging through the papers as they spill out on to the carpet.

— What are you doing, Am?

Ameliah doesn't look up, her hands burrowing into the suitcase, pushing more and more letters and photos out of her way.

— There's a clipping, from the newspaper, from when Mum died. The accident.

— OK. And?

Ameliah turns her head and stares at Heather.

— I know I've seen his face before. There's a photo,

with the story, there's people there, just standing. I've just got a feeling.

Heather leaves the bed and kneels down next to Ameliah.

— What are you saying, Am?

Ameliah pushes papers aside more frantically until the bottom of the suitcase comes into view.

— What if he was there?

Heather's eyes widen.

— What do you mean? When she died?

Ameliah stops digging.

— It's not here. Yeah. When she died. What if he was there, Heather?

She sits back on her feet and lets out a sigh. Heather crosses her legs.

— I don't know what you're saying. You think he knows something about the accident?

Ameliah can feel the pulse in her neck as she stares at Heather.

— I don't know.

Ryan stared up the garden. Nathan lowered the stick in his right hand, the ball still trapped under his left. The two of them stood facing each other, a garden length apart, like cowboys ready to draw. Ryan felt his fingers twitch by his hip with a sense of purpose. Mum said doing the right thing makes you powerful.

He imagined pulling a gun at lightning speed and shooting Nathan down before he could get his pistol out of its holster.

— What do you want, weed?

The slight slope of the garden gave Nathan even more of a height advantage. His long shadow stretched out towards Ryan on the patchy lawn.

— You know you don't always have to try and talk like a wrestler?

Ryan inflated his chest, as much for himself as for Nathan, then tucked his thumbs into the front of his baggy jeans, like he was the sheriff chatting to his townspeople.

— You OK?

Nathan looked shocked.

— What? Get lost, man.

He dropped the ball and started rolling it left and right with his foot. Ryan walked towards him.

— Fair play for saying bullshit.

Nathan carried on dribbling the ball as Ryan got closer.

— Last time I swore, I got grounded for a week.

He stopped spitting distance from Nathan. Nathan trapped the ball dead under his right foot and looked at him.

— It is bullshit. I'm not going. They can't make me.

Ryan shrugged.

— They kinda can.

Nathan leaned forward and Ryan lifted his hands.

— I'm just saying. Look, I don't want to go any more than you do, but it's happening. Just the thought of being stuck in some crappy caravan with them makes me want to throw up.

— They make me sick. Holding hands at the table—

Nathan stopped himself, his guard still up. Ryan looked at him and for a split second thought Nathan might cry. Nathan scowled.

— Yeah, well, I'm gonna make sure that it's the worst trip ever.

He spun round and booted the ball at the back fence. The crack of leather against the thin wooden panel rang round the garden. Ryan scratched his head.

— You know, we could make it easier for each other.

The ball trickled past Nathan as he turned back to Ryan and rolled to the right of Ryan's feet. Nathan stared at him.

— What are you talking about?

Ryan stuck out his right foot and dragged the ball back towards him under his toes. In one move he rolled it up on to his

160

foot and flicked it up into his hands. He stood proudly with the ball under his arm.

— I'm talking about being a little bit more clever with it.

Nathan looked surprised.

— Since when do you know how to control a ball?

Ryan smiled.

— I know a lot of stuff, Nathan.

He threw the ball at Nathan's body with a snap of his arm. Nathan adjusted himself just in time, catching the ball against his chest with a thud. He took a step back to steady himself and smiled a reluctant smile.

— Can you keep it up?

Ryan raised his eyebrows and nodded in reply. Nathan threw the ball up in an arc towards him. Ryan positioned his feet and headed the ball back with enough power and accuracy to reach Nathan's head perfectly. Nathan headed it back. Ryan controlled the ball on his chest and volleyed it softly. Nathan caught the ball and smiled.

— Well, who knew? How come you never play at school?

Ryan sighed.

— I used to. A lot. Just, I dunno, I stopped being into it, I guess.

— Who do you support?

Ryan shook his head.

— Nobody.

Nathan looked disappointed. Ryan tried to rescue it.

— Cantona. I like Eric Cantona.

Nathan's face lit up.

— He's amazing, right? My dad bought me the same boots as him when I got picked for the district. Did you see that lob the other week? When he just stood there and put his hands up.

Nathan drops the ball and sticks his arms up in the air, pulling his best nonchalant pout.

— He's a genius.

Ryan felt a strange feeling of pride. Like he'd cracked a code or something. Then, as he smiled, his brain reminded him who he was dealing with and not to get cocky. Nathan stared into space, clearly thinking. Ryan heard a back door open somewhere along the street.

— So what's your plan?

Ryan puffed out his cheeks.

— I don't have a plan. I just think that if we work together a bit, we can probably both get what we want.

He stepped forward, surprised by his own confidence.

— We leave tomorrow. We get to this caravan park. We hold it down, without fighting but not overdoing it. We check the place out and we decide what to do.

— To mess it up.

— No, well, yeah, maybe. Listen, what I'm saying is we play it cool and work out what makes sense together. If we work together, we'll be twice as powerful.

Nathan stared at him, like he was trying to see through his face into his brain. Ryan chewed the inside of his lip, waiting, unsure whether Nathan would agree or just punch him in the stomach.

— OK.

Nathan nodded. Ryan felt his eyes widen.

— OK?

— Yeah, OK. But this doesn't change anything. You're still a weed.

Ryan nodded.

— OK, Hulk Hogan.

Nathan tossed him the ball and started walking inside. Ryan felt the old leather against his palms. Looking down at the ball, he got a kick of nostalgia. He turned to Nathan.

— Where are you going?

Nathan turned round, walking backwards towards the house.

— If we're gonna do this properly, we need to start level. I'm gonna say sorry. Gotta let 'em think they're running the show, right?

He fired a pretend gun with his finger.

— Oh yeah, the other day, when you forgot your key? Your bum chum phoned. He said you should call him back.

He turned and walked into the house.

Ryan looked back at the ball in his hands. He wasn't completely sure what had just happened. His gut told him he might have started something that would ultimately end badly, but even knowing that, he couldn't help feeling proud to have held his own. Whatever happened, that was easily the longest interaction he'd ever had with Nathan that didn't end up with him in a headlock.

He thought about Liam, probably phoning up to apologise for his big mouth.

He smiled to himself and let go of the ball, using his right foot to keep it up. He circled around on the grass, juggling the ball between his feet. He needed to let Liam know they were going away. Liam wasn't going to be happy. Ryan felt the ball travelling forward, out of his control. He lunged with his left leg, trying to hook it as he fell. His weaker foot connected way too hard with the ball, sending it looping up and away from him.

He froze as he watched it fly like a cannonball diagonally over the back fence into the garden of the house next to the one opposite.

He felt his breakfast churn inside him as he stood up. Nathan's ball was gone. Nathan would not be happy. Ryan had to get it back.

He moved to the top corner of the garden and tried to see through the crack where the fences met. Through the tiny slit he could make out long green grass, much thicker and greener than their lawn, like it hadn't been cut for a long time. He couldn't see the ball.

Taking a step back, he looked at the fence. It was taller than him, but he reckoned he could get his hands on to the top edge. The question was whether he could pull his own body weight up and, if he managed that, would the old fence take his weight before he jumped off?

He looked back at the house. No sign of anyone. Nathan was probably in the living room right now, standing in front of Dad and Sophia, performing his fake apology.

Ryan looked up at his bedroom window. In the shadow of the roof the glass looked lifeless. For a second he imagined himself looking down. He thought about how weird that would be, if the ghost of someone showed up before that person had even died.

He told himself that someone had already had that idea and he was just remembering a film; he knew he did that all the time.

Turning back to the fence, he breathed in deeply.

— You're doing this. You're doing this now.

He closed his eyes and when he opened them he was hanging from the fence, the thin edge of the wooden panel digging into the soft pads of his fingers. He felt the muscles in his stomach straining as he tried to pull his body up. A weird shooting pain shot down his legs as he strained, kicking out towards the side fence. His left foot gripped the top edge, propping him up like some badly made human suspension bridge across the corner where the two fences met.

He composed himself and shuffled his hands towards the corner, feeling his weight lighten as his legs took more of the strain.

Then he was up. Sitting on the corner. The plus sign of conjoined fences under his thighs, his right leg hanging in his garden, his left in the garden diagonally across.

The ball was nestled in the thick grass of the other lawn two body lengths from the fence. Ryan looked down at the ground. He was sure jumping off wouldn't be a problem, but if getting back up was going to be as much of a strain again, he'd need a minute to get ready and, if someone came to the back door or window, that was a minute he might not have.

He looked up the other garden to the back of the house. The deep red bricks lightened towards the top. He thought about those glass tubes you get from the seaside with the different coloured sand in layers.

He stared at the white back door. He couldn't make out any activity inside.

There's no one in. You don't have a problem. Just do it.

He swung his right leg over so both his feet hung in the other garden. Lifting his body weight on to his hands, he saw the white back door open. Too late to stop, he felt the fence sway as he pushed off. As he jumped forward, the waistband of his jeans caught in the fence. He felt himself falling head first, the realisation dropping in his gut, his waist pinned to the wood. As the blood rushed to his head, he raised his hands and looked up, trying to brace himself for the impact. Then he saw her.

— Maybe he'll come round again?

Heather lifts her arms above her head and moves on to her tiptoes, pretending to be a ballerina. The oversized red and black checked shirt hangs off her like a cloak. Ameliah watches her turn then give up in pain.

— Yeah. Maybe.

As she speaks, her mind tries to picture the newspaper article, the black inky type on that dirty off-white paper, the dots of the printed monochrome picture, the policemen, the tape, the witnesses. She tries to picture Joe.

Heather leans forward, her hands on her knees.

— Come on, Am, let's do something. We can't just stay in here all day.

Ameliah gives up on the image in her head and looks down at herself in the old chunky blue and black lumberjack shirt. She tries to picture Mum in it, younger, sitting on her bed. Heather picks up a dark blue sweater from the floor and starts pulling it on over the shirt. The thick material buries her. The words Naf Naf are emblazoned across the chest in pink and white block letters.

— This stuff is so big.

Heather sticks her arms out either side like a scarecrow.

— This would fit my brother! How did they even know who was a girl and who was a boy?

Ameliah watches Heather but pictures Joe. She

thinks about Nan holding up the piece of paper with his address and her eyes widen.

— Can you hear my nan?

She sits forward, turning her ear to the open bedroom door. Heather listens too. The house is quiet. Heather shakes her head.

— I can't hear anything.

Ameliah stands up.

— She must be asleep. I can probably get a look at it without waking her up.

— Get a look at what?

Heather starts to rummage in the bin bag.

— His address, on the bit of paper, the one he gave her.

— What are you talking about, Am?

Ameliah stands in the bedroom doorway, looking along the landing at Nan's bedroom door.

— Shh. Wait here. I'll be back in a second.

— What are you doing?

— The paper.

Heather shrugs and sits on the floor as Ameliah tiptoes out on to the landing, treading on the edges where the carpet meets the skirting board.

As she gets to Nan's door, she leans in, resting her ear against the painted wood. There's the light sound of Nan's breathing, not quite a snore, but heavy enough to say she's probably asleep.

Ameliah reaches for the round doorknob, turning slowly. The tendons in her fingers push out under her skin like tiny ropes, taut from the tightness of her grip.

The door lightly clicks as she eases it open. There's the smell of soap power and old perfume.

Nan is asleep on her back on top of the white double bedspread. Next to her an old photo album lies open. The plastic film covering the pictures catches the dulled light coming through the curtains.

Ameliah scans the room. Books are stacked up in piles around the walls like a model skyline. An old fireplace sits lifeless and black, its grille grey with a layer of dust.

The bed frame is brass and old and makes Ameliah think of servants and maids and bedpans. She looks at the bedside table nearest to her. Nan's mobile phone lies on top of her purse. Sandwiched in between them, the white folded paper sticks out.

Ameliah looks at Nan. Her head tilted to one side,

her chin up like a cat. Her right hand rests on her chest, rising and falling with each breath. Her left hand is next to the photo album, as though she dropped off while looking through it. Ameliah looks at the upside-down page and makes out a teenage girl in baggy clothes.

Nan stirs and Ameliah holds her breath, looking back to the bedside table. She waits for Nan's breathing to fall back into its soft pattern and then takes a step forward, propping the door open behind her with her left foot.

Leaning in, she teases the folded paper from between the phone and purse. It feels thicker than she imagined between her fingers, like part of a page torn from an expensive notebook. She unfolds it and stares at the black writing. His letters are all capitals, clear but obviously written quickly. She reads the address again, mouthing the words, burning the information into her brain.

Underneath the address he has just written the word Joe. No surname.

Ameliah feels her face scrunch up as she reads it.

A car goes past outside. She folds the paper up again and slides it back between the purse and phone, leaving it sticking out just as much as it was.

171

She glances at Nan then at the photo album as she reverses her movements out of the room.

As she clicks the door shut, Ameliah whispers the address to herself, repeating it again and again as she walks back to her room.

Heather looks up at her from the floor next to the black bag. She's wearing a red beanie hat.

— Happy?

Ameliah heads straight to her bedside table and picks up the shoebox lid and her pen, mouthing the address to herself.

Heather stands up and moves towards the bed. Ameliah stares at the address on the brown card in her lap, her skin charged with her idea.

— I think it's by the high street. On the way to town.

Heather sits down next to her and looks at the shoebox lid.

— So what? We track him like stalkers?

Ameliah pushes the lid down between her bed and the table. She looks at Heather and nods, biting her bottom lip.

— Exactly.

INDEX

B

CHAPTER 6

Ryan feels cool air on his skin and opens his eyes. He's standing in a lush garden, plants and flowers and trees all around him. Looking down, he sees he's naked except for a green star-shaped leaf covering his privates. The morning sun is warm on his skin.

He feels a hand in his and, looking across, he sees Eve standing next to him with three of the same star leaves covering her bits. His Eve. The green-eyed girl from two gardens away. She's smiling. He feels amazing. He looks at Eve, Eve looks at him and they're holding hands and nodding their heads while all around them the huge plants with their multicoloured flowers sway to the sounds of A Tribe Called Quest.

— Ryan. Ryan. Are you OK?

Ryan heard her voice and opened his eyes. He saw her blurred edges. His whole body ached and his left knee felt like it had been twisted all the way round.

173

He could feel the soft grass under his back as he stared up. Her upside-down face came into focus.

— Are you OK? Wait here, don't move.

Ryan tried to sit up and felt his ribs dig into his lungs.

He reached down and felt his blood turn cold as he touched the naked skin of his thighs. Where were his jeans?

He felt pain across his chest as he propped himself up on to his elbows and looked down at his body. Following his naked legs down to his ankles he saw that his jeans, turned inside out, were covering his feet and stretching up to the fence where they were trapped at the waist, wedged into a split in the wooden panels.

The fall must've pulled them off but they got stuck on his trainers. He looked down at his crotch. His white briefs were still in place. He told himself that was something. At least she hadn't seen everything. Was this her garden? He had to get away. How could this be happening?

He sat up fully, feeling pain as he breathed in. He turned to look back at the house. The white back door was open and he could see into the dark kitchen. He couldn't make out Eve or anyone else. He shuffled towards the fence on his backside and starting pulling at his jeans, trying to tug them loose from the fence. They wouldn't move. His shoes were wedged inside the ankles of the denim, trapping him. He started to panic, pulling more violently. The fence rattled, but the waistband of his jeans wouldn't come loose.

Ryan could feel his heart starting to pound in his chest and sweat forming on his forehead.

— Come on. *Come on*!

— What are you doing?

Eve kneeled beside him, easing his body back on to the grass. Her hand on his chest felt cool and calm. He looked up at her.

She smiled and held up a large pair of scissors.

— I'm gonna have to cut them.

Ryan felt his face torn between smiling and wanting to cry. Her voice was like a memory. His head was spinning and he felt like he might pass out at any moment. He moved his hands, pulling his grey jumper down, trying to cover his pants.

— I'm sorry. I was coming for my ball. My pants and, is this—?

Eve smiled and shook her head.

— Shut up. Tell me inside. Now hold still.

— What time is it?

— I dunno.

— Check your phone.

Heather pulls out her sleek mobile and taps the screen.

— 16:07, Sarge.

— Stop joking about.

Ameliah tries to see through the bush.

— Do you think he's in there now?

Heather taps her phone screen. Ameliah narrows her eyes.

— I don't know. Maybe. Maybe not.

— Can we go now?

— No.

Heather reads something on her phone.

— Look, Simone and them are going to the park. Let's go, Am. I'm bored.

Ameliah stares through the bush at the black and white building. She looks at the upstairs bay window. The net curtains prevent anyone seeing in. Heather holds up her phone close to Ameliah's face.

— Am, let's go and meet them.

Ameliah shakes her head.

— We need to wait. He might come out.

Heather puts her phone back in her pocket.

— Yeah, and then what? We follow him? Where to exactly? We've been here ages. Let's go.

Ameliah's eyes don't leave the building.

— You go. I'll be fine.

Heather slaps her shoulder.

— Oi. This is stupid. Let's go — detective work is boring. You said yourself you're not even sure he was in that photo.

Ameliah stares straight ahead.

— I'm not going anywhere.

— No? So what, you're just gonna stand here like some kind of weirdo and wait to see him? Maybe follow him to the chippy? He's just some guy, Am.

Ameliah doesn't move. Heather blows air out of her cheeks and shakes her head.

— Fine. You waste your time playing private detective if you want, I'm going.

Ameliah doesn't look at her.

— You know you're hard work sometimes, Am, you really are. Call me later, yeah?

She walks away, back towards the building. Ameliah watches her go. As Heather passes the drive, she glances back at the bush, pulls a face then turns to the house and sticks her middle finger up at it. Ameliah stares up at the upstairs bedroom window, looking for any sign of a response.

Ryan looked round the room and realised the layout of the house was an exact mirror image of his own, with the kitchen on the opposite side. He could still feel the ache in his chest as he sat on the edge of the deep brown sofa with a towel wrapped around his legs.

On the wall above the fireplace he saw a silver-framed photograph of a stern-looking man with dark hair and olive skin in military uniform. He knew this must be Eve's nan's house. Liam had told him she was staying with her nan, but on the next street up? With a back garden that touched theirs? Ryan felt his stomach dancing as he heard Eve close the fridge.

— Do you want the spoon with it?

Her voice called from the kitchen and Ryan imagined Mum, chopping potatoes, singing along to Billy Joel.

— Erm, yes please. I don't mind.

Eve walked in carrying two long glasses full of strawberry Nesquik. The handle of a silver spoon stuck out from the top of both. She handed him one and sat in the armchair to his right.

— I like to use the spoon. That way it lasts longer.

Ryan shifted his weight in his seat.

— Thanks. I'm sorry.

— Stop saying that.

Eve smiled and slurped a spoonful of pink milk.

— How old are you?

He could feel her eyes on him.

— Thirteen, I mean, yeah, I'm thirteen. How 'bout you?

Eve slurped another spoonful.

— I'm fourteen next week.

— Cool.

Ryan took a swig and felt the cool milk wash against his top lip.

Eve lifted her feet up and tucked them underneath her on the chair as she drank. Ryan noticed a small collection of freckles near the top of her left arm. Like a constellation.

— You're freckly.

Eve looked confused.

— What?

Ryan pointed.

— On your arm. You have freckles.

Eve looked at her arm and covered the freckles with her hand. Ryan shook his head.

— Freckles are good. I love freckles.

He closed his eyes.

— I'm sorry. I don't know what I'm talking about.

Eve looked at him like she knew him from somewhere.

— You and your friend have a habit of saying the wrong thing, don't you?

— My friend? Oh, you mean Liam.

Eve nodded.

— Yeah, well, pretty much. I'm sorry I stared at your freckles.

— Stop saying sorry.

Eve lifted her glass and finished the last of her milk.

— And you've got freckles too.

She pointed at the towel covering Ryan's legs. Ryan felt the blood rushing to his face. Eve smiled.

— It's like a film or something.

Ryan held his hands in his lap as he looked at her.

— *Back to the Future.*

Eve smiled.

— Yeah.

She stood up and moved towards him.

— I guess the universe wanted us to meet. Glass?

He looked up at her. Her white vest clung to her body and Ryan tried to avoid staring at her chest.

— The universe?

Eve blew air out of her mouth.

— Gimme your glass, Freckly.

Ryan smiled nervously and held it out. Eve took it and walked towards the kitchen.

— My nan will be home soon so you might want to go before she gets here.

Ryan stared at her. She nodded at the towel. Ryan stood up, holding it in place with a tight grip.

— Yeah. Course. Sorry, I mean, yeah.

Eve smiled as she walked into the kitchen.

— You don't talk to girls much, do you?

Ryan stared at the military man in the photograph and imagined Eve's nan as some strongly built military wife who would pull the arms off any boy she found in his pants alone with her granddaughter in her living room.

He walked into the kitchen. Eve stood at the sink rinsing the glasses.

— Maybe I should go back over the fence?

He stared out of the back door into the garden. On the small concrete patio his jeans lay, one leg cut from the ankle to the hip.

— You think that's wise, Evil Knievel?

Eve leaned against the sink. Light from the window lit her from behind. Ryan looked back into the living room.

— I don't fancy walking the streets in my pants.

— No? They're quite nice pants.

Their eyes met and for a second Ryan forgot where he was. He imagined, if life was a film, this would be where he walked towards her slowly and she did the same and they'd meet in the middle of the kitchen and there was the sound of a key in the front door...

Eve's face dropped.

— Go. Now!

She pushed him out of the back door, pulling the towel away from his legs. Ryan stumbled on to the patio in his pants as the back door closed behind him. He looked down the garden, then at his butchered jeans, then back at the door. He had no idea what to do. The back door quickly opened and Eve's face appeared.

— Meet me by the fence later. Nine o'clock.

Then she was gone. Ryan stared at the door. He could make out the brushstrokes in the white gloss paint. Nine o'clock.

He grabbed his jeans and ran down the garden, scooping the ball up as he went. At the bottom, leaning against the fence, was a wheelbarrow, as if it had been placed there. Ryan smiled and threw his jeans and the ball over the fence. He jumped up on to the wheelbarrow and, using his hands as leverage, he threw his legs up and over the fence, landing on his feet in his own back garden.

He felt the pain in his back as he stood up, then, picking up his jeans, he walked towards his back door in his pants, beaming from ear to ear.

Ameliah feels the cold air on the back of her neck. She pulls her thick grey hood up over her curls and lets out a sigh. She has no idea what time it is, but the sun has moved behind the houses across the street and it feels like a while since Heather left. The backs of her legs ache from standing for so long and she can feel hunger bubbling in her stomach.

She thinks about Heather, in the park with Simone and the others, talking about girly things and tapping their phones. She wonders whether Heather made up an excuse for her not being there. Whether anyone even asked.

A double-decker bus rolls past and Ameliah spots the same advert for holidays in Turkey she has seen three times already. She shakes her head and looks down. Nan will be worried about where she is. She didn't leave a note and doesn't have a phone. She looks back through the bush at the building, resigning herself to leave, and then Joe steps out of the front door.

At first she keeps her distance, staying two lamp posts away as she follows him along the pavement of the main road but, as he turns on to the high street, the safety of scattered strangers and the fading sun make her feel like she can get closer.

She remembers a cartoon with a hunter following a rabbit, him disappearing behind a tree every time the rabbit turned round. She makes sure to look into shop windows, as though she's interested in buying something.

He moves with purpose and she has to skate between people to keep up. His brown workman's jacket makes him seem younger somehow as he walks through the sliding glass doors of the supermarket.

Picking up an empty basket, she watches him turn round the far end of the fruit and vegetables aisle. She hangs back, moving past the end of the aisle and peering round the corner of the next. He walks straight past it so she shuffles up the aisle to make sure she stays behind him.

Ameliah can feel her heart beating as she moves past

stacked boxes of cereal and it hits her that she has no idea what she's doing. She remembers begging Dad to let her sit in the trolley when they went shopping, him telling her she was too big now, shaking his head, then giving in and lifting her into the mesh cage. A smooth green melon cool in her lap as Dad steered around, speaking their shopping list out loud to remind himself.

— Careful, dear.

The old lady lays her hand on Ameliah's shoulder, stopping them from colliding. Ameliah snaps out of her daydream, scanning the aisle both ways over the old lady's shoulder.

— Are you OK? You look lost.

Ameliah feels herself start to panic.

— What? No. I'm fine. Where did he go?

— Where did who go, love?

The old lady shakes her head as Ameliah walks away from her, moving past the tea bags. She jogs along the end of the aisles, looking down each one. He's not in any of them. She squeezes her fists as she reaches the last one. Joe is halfway down, reading the label on a bottle of red wine. Ameliah stops, relieved. He looks up. She ducks quickly back round the corner, her face

185

right next to bottles of fizzy drinks. Did he see her? She tells herself he can't have and presses her hand against her chest to calm down.

From behind the crisps she watches Joe lay his items on the conveyer belt at the till. She makes out two bottles of wine, a large pizza and what looks like a bottle of shampoo. He must be on his own. She remembers the lack of wedding ring.

The girl on the till is smiling and trying to chat to him, but he seems oblivious.

He's planning a pizza and wine night. Maybe a film. She tries to think what kind of film he's going to watch. Something about spies. Something old, with car chases through arty European streets. As he hands the woman his card to pay, he looks back straight towards her. Ameliah jumps and feels a large multipack of crisps slip off the shelf next to her. The pack behind it starts to fall, causing a crisp packet avalanche on to the floor. People start to look towards her as she hides from him, her back against the shelves, breathing deeply.

A figure wearing a dark supermarket polo shirt appears from nowhere and starts to pick up the crisps.

— Are you OK?

His voice is warm and seems too low for his slight body. She looks down at his arms as he scoops up the rustling packets. The hairs on them are dark against his pale skin.

— I've told them the shelves need edges, you know?

Ameliah knows it's him, even before he looks up at her and smiles an awkward smile. His eyes are dark in his lean face. The same face she remembers staring at across the park. Without his cap she can see the waves in his thick black hair. She feels her stomach getting warm as she notices the faint beginnings of a moustache.

— Sorry. I'm clumsy.

The boy stands up and starts to stack the crisp packets back on the shelf.

— No problem. Do I know you?

His eyes are the colour of dark coffee-table wood. Swirling brown as he glances at her again. She stares. The boy smiles and she notices his two front teeth are crooked. He tilts his head and she feels the urge to put her hand against his face. She fights it and instead tilts her own head, mirroring his action.

— You look familiar.

Ameliah opens her mouth to tell him she's the girl

from the park, that she saw him and he saw her, but then over his shoulder she sees Joe walk out through the exit. Her head snaps back up.

— I've gotta go.

The boy looks confused as she pushes past him and starts to run towards the exit, not turning round as he says his name.

— It's me. Ryan, who'd you think? I know, Nathan just told me. I didn't know. I dunno, you know what he's like. Yeah. Don't worry about it. Liam, seriously, it's fine. Yeah, but I still shouldn't have run off, that was stupid, look it doesn't matter. I saw her. Yes. Today. Earlier. In her garden. Yeah. No, back garden. It's a long story. Yo, she lives on the next street! Up from ours. OK, her nan lives on the next street. Yeah. Their garden backs on to ours. I know. What? Shut up, man. Stop saying that, seriously, you sound like Macho Man Randy Savage or something. I know, but check this, I'm meeting her tonight. Yeah. Nine o'clock. I know, two hours. Cos she told me to, I mean I want to. Look, are you listening to what I'm saying? I know. Who's that? Is it Jason? What's he got? Will he let you copy it? Listen, stop changing the subject. I'm

188

meeting her tonight. I don't know, it won't matter, she won't be able to see me anyway. Cos she'll be on the other side of the fence. It doesn't matter. I'll speak to you tomorrow. Nathan's waiting for his dad to call. Yeah. OK. All right, cool. What? No I'm not saying that. Because it's disgusting. Look, I'm going. No, bye, Liam. Bye.

— You're thirteen years old, young lady.

— I know how old I am.

— Oh, you do? That's good, well, maybe you should spend some time thinking about what that means.

— I said I'm sorry. It's not even that late.

— That's not the point, Ameliah, and it is late. I didn't know where you were.

— I know, Nan. I got distracted. I'm here now.

Nan sighs from the edge of the sofa. Her face is pale in the dark room. Streetlight through the still open curtains turns the edges of the furniture orange.

— It's not fair, Am. You of all people should know that – anything could've happened.

— OK, but it didn't.

— But it could have.

Ameliah rolls her eyes. Nan sighs.

— Am, please, don't tell me you can't understand what I'm saying. After your rudeness this morning, and now this? You know you're in the wrong here.

— I get it, Nan. You're angry. I'm sorry. Can I go now?

Nan closes her eyes.

— Give me strength.

Her eyes open.

— You should have told me. You should have let me know. My mind ran towards all sorts of horrible things.

Ameliah shrugs and looks down at the living-room carpet. Nan stands up.

— After what we've been through, don't you think it was wrong not to let me know?

Ameliah feels her body tense up.

— Wrong? What about you?

She stares up at Nan. Nan frowns.

— What about me?

— You! Just letting some guy in. Who knows who he is? He could be anyone, Nan, but you're all like, yeah, come in, can I make you breakfast? It's so nice of you to come, say hello to the man, Ameliah, he knew your dad, Ameliah.

— That's not what it was. I—

— He could be anyone! He turns up here, mentions Dad and we're just supposed to welcome him in?

— You're overreacting, love.

Nan puts her hand on Ameliah's shoulder. Ameliah shrugs it off.

— And what about Richard?

Nan's face straightens as she lowers her arm.

— What about him?

Ameliah shrugs.

— Who the hell is he? What the hell does he want?

— What do you mean what does he want? He wants to be my friend. He wants to—

— Your friend? Jesus, Nan, I'm not five years old.

Nan stares at Ameliah.

— You listen to me, young lady, and I mean listen. Richard is a friend who I like and who I enjoy spending time with and if I choose to spend time with him I will. My business is my business and you better remember who you're talking to.

— Yeah, well, Mum wouldn't like it.

Nan's face drops. Ameliah feels her words sit at shoulder height in the air between them. Her stomach turns as she waits for Nan to explode. Her mind runs the lines she expects Nan to speak, but Nan says nothing. Her chest deflates as she looks at Ameliah then she walks out of the room.

— *Psssssst.* What are you doing?

The fence spoke in a voice that felt too light and warm for a fence. Ryan looked over his shoulder. The back door was fully closed. He looked at the lawn. The light from the kitchen projected a yellow rectangle on to the dark grass.

— Ryan.

The fence tried hard to whisper. Ryan started to walk towards it, glancing back at the house, checking the living-room curtains were closed. He knew Sophia and Dad were inside.

— I'm here.

He felt his face contort into a weird shape as he tried to keep his voice down.

— I can see that, dummy. Come closer.

The voice came from the crack in the corner where the fences met. Ryan couldn't see Eve and it felt unfair that she could see him.

— I can't see you.

He stared at the crack, his eyes trying to make out a sliver of her body.

— It's your eyes. They take time to adjust to the light. I've been here for a bit.

Ryan heard her voice move and knew she was sitting down. He did the same, facing the corner like he'd been told off.

— Did you get over the fence OK?

— Yeah. Thanks for the wheelbarrow.

— That's OK. I figured a pair of trousers was enough damage for one day.

Ryan felt himself blush. He looked down at the back of his hands. His skin looked pale against the dark of his jumper sleeve.

— Sorry again, about earlier I mean.

Eve tapped the other side of the fence.

— Stop saying sorry. It sounds like you don't mean it.

Ryan opened his mouth then stopped himself saying it again.

— Thanks. For helping me.

— How's your chest?

— It's fine.

Ryan pressed his palm against his chest and felt the dull ache.

— Was your nan OK?

— Yeah. She had no idea. We did pretty well. Is that your house?

Ryan looked back at it. The kitchen light had been left on. The living-room curtains were closed and still, a slight pink glow coming from inside. Upstairs, Dad's window and his looked black, set into the dark bricks.

— Yeah. Kind of. That's my room upstairs. Are you at the back too?

— Yeah. How far away from each other do you think we sleep?

Ryan looked through the gap up at the back of Eve's nan's house and the upstairs bedroom window. He tried to picture her standing in the window.

— I'd say about half a football pitch.

There was a pause. Then she spoke.

— That's good to know.

— So where are your mum and dad?

— They're back in Dublin. I'm staying with Nan for the holidays.

Ryan sat silently, brushing the thin grass with his fingers. He pictured her sitting in the same position on the other side of the wood.

— They're getting a divorce.

Ryan felt her staring. Even though he knew she couldn't see him fully, he could feel her eyes.

— It's pretty rubbish.

There was a pause.

— My mum died, I mean, she's dead. I guess it's kind of the same thing, right?

Eve laughed. Like a quieter version of Mum.

— I'm sorry. That's horrible, it's just the way you said it. I didn't mean—

Ryan felt his heart beating.

— It's fine. I do that, say stupid stuff I mean.

Eve laughed some more.

— I know. I like it.

Ryan felt his face tingle. Eve stopped laughing.

— How did she die?

He felt his face drop. He ran through the responses he'd trained himself to give to strangers and teachers and parents of schoolmates.

— She got sick. It was a couple of years ago now.

He prayed that Eve would hear in his voice to leave it there.

— So you're thirteen, right?

The relief at the change of subject was swiftly followed by the sinking realisation that he was a year younger. Being in the year below was a big obstacle. He considered lying then remembered that she already knew.

— Yeah. Unlucky for some.

— I can't wait till my birthday. Fourteen sounds so much better, don't you reckon?

Ryan leaned his head against the fence.

— Totally.

— You wanna come? On my birthday I mean? It's on Wednesday. Have some cake?

Ryan answered without thinking.

— Yeah. Yes please. I love cake. What kind of cake?

— I don't know. Does it matter?

— No. No it doesn't. Oh no, I can't.

There was a pause.

— OK. Don't worry about it.

— No, no, I want to, it's just that we're leaving on this stupid caravan holiday tomorrow to please my dad and my stepmum.

— Stepmum?

— Sophia. She's not so bad. I mean she's not some evil witch like in fairy tales or something. It's Nathan who's evil.

— Who's Nathan?

— He's her son.

— So your stepbrother?

— Yeah.

— Oh.

— Yeah. We leave in the morning, some beach in Devon. Five days. Will Mary come over, for cake I mean?

— Yeah, I think my mum's getting the ferry back too, but I'm not sure.

They both heard a rustling. Ryan sat up straight and looked around. He heard Eve get on to her knees.

— What was that?

— I dunno, where did it come from?

— My left.

They both jumped as the smoky-grey cat jumped up and clawed its heavy body on to the top of the fence. Eve sighed.

— Jesus!

Ryan tried to play it cool.

— It's the cat.

— I know, Ryan. Is it yours?

Ryan looked at the cat; its dark fur made it seem even fatter than it was. Its smug eyes flashed yellow.

— Nobody knows who owns it. Everyone feeds it, that's why it's so fat.

— Fat cat.

— Exactly.

They both laughed. Ryan thought about women in films visiting their husbands in jail, pressing their hands together either side of the glass.

— Look at the moon.

Eve's voice brought him back. Ryan looked up and saw the moon. It looked like someone had shaved the side off a frisbee made of pearl. He thought about saying that out loud then decided it sounded rubbish.

— Weird that there are people who've actually been there, don't you think?

He could tell by her voice that she was gazing up at it. The fact that she would even think a thought like that made Ryan feel like he would happily melt into the cold lawn.

— All the time. Imagine being on the dark side of it. What that would feel like.

— Lonely.

Ryan nodded, forgetting that she couldn't see him, as he stared up and imagined them both on the moon in NASA spacesuits, holding hands, bouncing massive slow-motion steps, laughing inside their helmets. He thought about the universe and Dad telling him how it has no edge.

— It's massive, isn't it?

— What is?

— Space. The universe I mean.

He stared up at the black sky, waiting for the stars to show themselves.

— And here we are, sitting in the corner of two gardens on a street on one of a whole bunch of planets.

— Yeah.

Ryan felt the warmth of sharing a thought and not having it shot down. He told himself he would happily sleep exactly where he was.

— I should go. Nan's gonna notice I'm not in my room.

Ryan heard Eve stand up. He got to his feet. Something about the light, or maybe the slight slope of the garden, made him feel taller than normal.

— I like speaking to you, Ryan. I'm glad the universe made you show me your pants.

Her mouth was right next to the wood and he could tell she was smiling. Ryan felt an urge to try and touch her, just for a second.

— Me too, I mean speaking and the pants.

Eve laughed.

— Enjoy your trip. Bring me a shell or something.

She started to walk away.

— Wait!

Ryan reminded himself to whisper.

— Do you like music?

Eve turned back.

— What do you mean?

Ryan leaned into the corner, his face touching the wood as he spoke through the crack.

— You like music, right?

— Everybody likes music, Ryan. See you later.

She smiled then turned and walked towards her back door. Ryan watched her through the crack, the light from the kitchen outlining her body as she opened the door and stepped inside.

Ryan turned round, leaning his back against the fence. The night air felt cool as he breathed in deeply.

— I like speaking to you, Ryan.

Saying the words out loud made them concrete. He felt like he was wearing body armour as he walked back down the garden towards the house. As he reached the back door, he thought he saw the flash of something move up in his bedroom window. He stared up at the glass. The moonlight turned it into a still mirror. He told himself it was nothing as he stepped inside.

The house is quiet. Nan is in her room. The echoes of the tension from before are still floating around. Ameliah imagines Nan earlier, sitting waiting for her on the sofa while she was out tracking Joe, trying to stay calm, her thumbs wrestling her fingers against her palms.

She thinks about Mum. When Mum was mad, the whole house felt different. Like somebody had fed a hosepipe through the letter box and was slowly poisoning them with some kind of deadly invisible gas. Now Ameliah knows where she got it from.

She stares at the small mobile phone in her hands. The black charger lead snakes away over the side of the bed next to her towards the plug as she lies on her back on top of the duvet. She can see the small battery icon in the top right-hand corner filling and re-filling in three stages, like somebody's pouring pixelated ink into it.

On the bedside table next to the stereo speaker, the old shell sits like a button.

Reaching out, Ameliah presses it with her finger. She feels the blood leave her fingertip as the shell refuses to give way. She makes a muffled explosion sound with her

201

mouth, as though she's pressed the button that launches a thousand missiles.

She moves her hand and presses play on the tape deck.

The speakers hum then, as the warm audience applause starts, she rolls back on to her back, the phone still in her hand.

She closes her eyes and listens. She remembers Dad saying that nothing is silent. That there is always some kind of sound on some level. He said that some scientists made a booth that they thought was completely soundproof, that blocked out every single external noise, but when people got in it, it was that quiet they could hear their own heart beating. So the only true silence was the space between heartbeats.

The man's gravelly voice through the speakers cracks as he sings, like he's almost shouting, but quietly somehow.

Ameliah pictures Dad at work, standing in front of his students, talking about science, and wonders whether they thought he was some stuffy science professor guy. They probably did. His dark wiry hair like a bonfire, his clever-clogs glasses, his pastel jackets.

She wonders if they ever saw him laughing, or doing his impression of the Terminator, or yelping like a little dog when he spilled his coffee down his shirt.

The brushed drums skip into the song's chorus. Ameliah leans over and turns the volume down. The music creeps lower. She thinks about babies inside their mothers. What the outside world must sound like. Dad was always reminding her how he and Mum played their favourite music to her before she was born. How he used to rest his headphones on either side of Mum's tummy as she lay down reading. Ameliah pictures him smiling, pressing his cheek to his shoulder, pretending to scratch a record. DJ Foetus.

Her body sinks further into the duvet as she lets the air out of her chest.

She pictures Joe, buying his wine and pizza, and imagines him lying on his bed on his own watching a film, the wine bottle sitting almost empty on his bedside table.

Was he in the photo from the newspaper? Did he know something about Mum?

She thinks about the voice from the tape and her

mind playing tricks. There's a reason she doesn't tell people everything.

— You don't even believe yourself, idiot.

Her mouth enjoys the words, her tongue clicking against the back of her teeth to over-pronounce the letter 't'.

She thinks about Heather, giving the middle finger to his flat as she walked away, and then she sees the boy's face from near the crisps, his dark eyes and his smile.

She jumps off the bed, landing like a cat on her toes between the scattered tapes and open shoeboxes, as the next song starts with more guitar and what sounds like a harp. She squats by the wall and digs into her schoolbag, pulling out a light green exercise book, then hops back to the bed like she's a burglar avoiding laser tripwires.

She presses and holds the circular button on top of the phone with her fingertip. The screen blinks on, flashing the company logo. She crosses her legs under her and uses her finger to keep her place as she reads a phone number written in red biro from the cover of the exercise book, pressing the phone number buttons with her thumb. She chooses save contact and types Heather's name.

The man on the tape repeats the same two words as the song fades.

Ameliah pictures Mum with her guitar and notebook, scribbling lyrics. She looks at the tapes on the floor and tells herself she needs to make some kind of table to note down what is on them all.

The small square screen seems too bright for its size as Ameliah clicks back to menu and selects contacts. She highlights Heather's name and chooses send message.

She smiles to herself, picturing the look on Heather's face in her room when she opens a message from her. The tiny buttons make it hard for her thumb not to make mistakes and she thinks about how fast Heather can tap out pretty much an essay.

She mouths the words as she types, saying sorry and that this will be her number. She feels powerful as she watches the small picture of an envelope pretend to fly off the screen.

The audience claps and whoops as the acoustic baseline of the next track plays.

Ameliah lies back down on her side, holding the

phone, looking at Heather's name under 999 in the contacts list. Her thumb scrolls down and up, highlighting one then the other. A phone with two numbers, her best friend and the emergency services.

I had a dream last night. I'm standing outside, next to a big road, like the dual carriageway that goes into town. I think maybe I'm waiting for a bus or something, but there's no bus stop and the road is dark. Not dark like the concrete grey of a normal road, I mean dark, like black. Like black tar, and it's smooth, and I look to my right and it's stretching off into the distance, but there are no cars and it's quiet and I can hear my name, like somebody saying my name, and I turn back and he's standing there. The boy with dark hair and brown eyes.

His face is thin and I can see the bones of his cheeks and there's something about him that makes me smile and he's saying my name and then he's smiling and he's holding out his hand. I'm looking down at his hand and his smooth fingers and I take his hand and his skin is lighter than my skin and my thumb rests on the soft bit between his thumb and first finger and I feel myself smiling and then it's like I'm getting lighter, like my body is floating upwards and the boy is still looking at me and smiling and he's floating up too and our feet lift off the ground and then I wake up. That's it. Weird, right? The weirdest thing is how real it felt. Like a memory rather than a dream. What's all that about?

I was going to tell Nan but I didn't. I wanted to tell you. On here. On your tape. I keep trying to picture you, you know, sitting on your bed back then, pressing the buttons, speaking your thoughts.

It would've been Mum's birthday, I mean it was her birthday. We were talking earlier, Nan and me, about birthdays. She remembered my eleventh, you remember? It's funny how somebody else's memory of the same thing can be so different.

I remember it.

I'm wearing Mum's old Nirvana T-shirt with the baby swimming on it. You saying eleventh is special because it's the same number next to itself and that's like rolling double six at snakes and ladders. It's one of those places that's supposed to feel American, they've got root beer and everything. You making Nan sing happy birthday twice, the waiter having to stand there and hold the cake.

The flames of the candles fighting to last. Watching you and Nan looking at each other. There's a pause and *you both look at me. I feel like I'm supposed to say something, like you want me to say something. I remember trying to replay all the birthdays I ever had in that moment, like one of those flick books with the pictures in the bottom corner of the page, but I can't.*

I picture Mum holding a cake she baked in both hands, you leaning in next to her and smiling. I try and remember you both telling me it's time to make a wish, to blow out the candles, but I can't for some reason and the waiter is waiting and I know his arm must be getting tired and you're standing there trying not to cry, Nan's forcing a smile and there's a space in between you where Mum should be.

CHAPTER 7

Ryan sat on the floor, his back against the sofa, watching the two muscular men grappling on the floor outside the ring. He decided that, even if it was fake, it still looked like hard work. Behind him, Nathan lay across the sofa, staring at the screen. Both of them wore jogging bottoms and T-shirts. The blond wrestler slammed the bigger man with the shaven head into the metal ringside steps.

— There's no way.

Nathan raised his hand in protest.

— He's gonna get whooped now.

Ryan looked up at Nathan, his face completely engrossed in the action.

— Come on! Get up!

Ryan imagined being in front of a crowd that big. A stadium packed with thousands of people chanting your name. He wondered whether that was what Nathan was thinking.

— He's gonna do the shoulder-breaker any minute, watch.

Nathan pointed at the screen. He noticed Ryan looking at him.

— Are you watching? I'm telling ya, shoulder-breaker, any minute.

— It's not real, you know.

Nathan looked at him. Ryan shrugged.

— I'm just saying.

Nathan shook his head.

— You're missing the point.

Ryan turned back to the screen as the bigger man lifted the blond man upside down over his shoulder. The blond man wriggled free and slipped down his back. Ryan thought about Liam, how he hadn't mentioned they were going away.

He felt eyes on him and looked up towards the kitchen.

Sophia stood in the doorway, smiling, her white T-shirt tucked into her stonewashed jeans.

— You boys hungry? Better get a good breakfast for the journey!

Nathan didn't look up.

— Yeah. I am, Mum.

Ryan smiled.

— Yes please, Sophia.

Sophia nodded.

— I'll make bacon sandwiches. Are you guys excited?

Ryan felt Nathan hold his breath behind him on the sofa. He kept a straight face.

— Yeah.

Sophia looked at Nathan.

— And you, Nath?

Nathan glanced at her.

— Yeah, can't wait. Loads of ketchup on mine, Mum.

Sophia raised her eyebrows.

— Can I hear some manners, please?

Nathan stared at the screen.

— Yes please, thank you please.

Sophia looked at Ryan, rolling her eyes. Ryan smiled a safe smile as she walked back into the kitchen. He looked at Nathan.

— Is that you trying?

He felt a sharp pain in his back as Nathan kicked him in between his shoulder blades.

— Shut up. I know what I'm doing.

He pointed at the screen as the bigger man dropped to his knees holding the blond man upside down. The blond man flopped on to the mat.

— Told you. Boom! All over.

Ryan shook his head.

— That would break your neck if it was real.

— Probably, and your point is?

Ryan sighed. Nathan snorted.

— Exactly.

Ryan watched the referee lift the arm of the bigger man.

— Have you packed?

— Course not.

Ryan looked at him. Nathan smiled, nodding towards the kitchen.

She does it. In fact, I wouldn't be surprised if she's packed for you too.

Ryan thought about Sophia in his room, going through his drawers, choosing clothes. He stood up. Nathan flicked channels with the remote control.

— What's wrong, don't want her finding your booby mags?

Ryan thought about Eve. He pictured the freckles near her shoulder.

— Earth to Ryan, yo!

— What? Shut up, man.

— You shut up and don't be getting all chummy with me when we're in the car, all right? We don't have to be boyfriend and girlfriend, OK?

Ryan looked at Nathan and thought about holding him upside

down over his shoulder, Nathan begging for mercy.

— Don't worry, Nath, I don't want that either.

He walked towards the kitchen as Nathan stopped flicking on VH1.

Standing next to the fridge, he watched Sophia at the cooker, pressing bacon against the pan with the back of a fork. He heard Mum's voice telling Dad not to use metal cutlery on the new pan as the meat sizzled. Sophia turned to him.

— Oh, Ryan. Do you want sauce on yours?

Ryan thought about Mum making Sunday dinner, Dad sharpening the knife to cut the chicken on the back step.

— Yes please.

Sophia smiled.

— Red?

— Brown.

Sophia turned back to the hob.

— OK. You can go sit down if you like. I'll bring them through.

Ryan wondered what Mum would've made of Sophia, if they'd just met through a friend or at work. He tried to picture them in the same room.

— I'll pack my own bag.

Sophia turned to look at him, her face confused.

— I mean I'd like to pack for myself, for the trip.

— OK, Ryan. I think that's a good idea. You should hurry up though, your dad wants to leave before ten.

He nodded and walked out of the kitchen, realising he hadn't needed to say anything at all.

Ameliah smells the bacon as she walks downstairs. The crackle of the meat in the frying pan competes with the Nina Simone coming from the portable radio speaker on the kitchen windowsill. Nan moves round the kitchen in her apron like a ballerina making breakfast. She smiles at Ameliah as she notices her in the doorway.

— Morning, love.

She twists in time with the music towards her and pecks a small kiss on Ameliah's cheek.

Ameliah squeezes the shell in her jeans pocket as she watches Nan twirl away, her arms up, dancing with an invisible partner.

Nina Simone holds a long note as Nan pulls the frying pan off the hob.

— I hope you're hungry.

Ameliah looks at the pile of stacked toast on the table, in between two empty plates and glasses full of orange juice. She slides her free hand into the front pocket of her hoody, feeling the phone vibrate against her stomach.

— Sit down, love, it's nearly ready.

Ameliah sits down at the table and takes a sip of orange juice, letting the cold liquid run around between her teeth and gums like mouthwash before she swallows.

Her hand grips the phone as she looks at Nan's back. The song finishes.

— There'll never be another Nina.

Nan lays the thick doorstep sandwich on the plate in front of her as Ameliah feels the phone vibrate again.

— Thanks, Nan. About last night, I'm—

— I know, love. Forget about it. There's sauce there if you want it.

She sits down with her own sandwich and swigs from her orange juice.

Ameliah takes the phone out of her pocket and lays it on the table.

Nan looks at the phone and for a second Ameliah

thinks she might have made a mistake. Nan smiles and takes a huge bite out of her sandwich.

— Good idea, love. Does it still work OK?

Ameliah nods and feels the relief in her shoulders.

— Yeah, seems to. Heather hasn't stopped sending me messages since I told her.

The phone vibrates again on cue. They both smile.

Ameliah looks at the phone screen. The dark letters say four new messages.

Nan takes another bite.

— It'll be nice to be able to reach you.

Ameliah watches her chewing like a horse and feels herself straighten up in her seat.

— She would've wanted you to have it. I mean to be able to know you were OK.

Ameliah stares at the stacked toast.

— Mum used to tell me how mad you got when she came in late.

She looks at Nan. Nan stops chewing. Ameliah looks down. Nan swallows her toast.

— I was quite strict.

She takes another bite and talks with her mouth full.

— I guess it came from my mum.

— Mum's nan?

— Yeah, she was an army wife, and you don't get much stricter than that. We moved around a lot so she always thought she had to keep me in check, stop me running off with any old boy.

Nan finishes her mouthful and smiles a cheeky smile.

— Didn't work though, did it?

Ameliah leans in.

— Why not?

Nan leans forward.

— Cos I ran off first chance I got, jumped on a boat to Ireland with a boy.

Ameliah's face lights up with excitement.

— So what happened?

Nan stares at the pile of toast and sighs.

— Just a boy, with a saxophone, but man could he play.

— Nan, what happened?

Nan snaps out of her daydream.

— I learned a lesson, that's what. Let's just say that not everyone gets a fairy tale like your mum and dad.

She takes another slice of toast.

— What do you say to us watching a film later? Your choice. We'll take the old one back and choose something for us tonight. Good idea?

Ameliah nods and picks at her sandwich with her fingers.

— Yeah. Good idea.

— Good then. I'm gonna be in the garden sorting out those borders. What are you up to?

— I thought I'd go through some more of the spare room.

— Good.

Nan pushes the last of her sandwich into her mouth and reaches for the top slice of toast. Ameliah pulls out the shell and lays it on the table next to her plate, looking up at Nan. Nan sees the shell and stops chewing. She looks at Ameliah. The long strings play out the end of the song.

— She'd want you to have that too.

She smiles and finishes her mouthful.

— Funny how something so small can be so important, don't you think?

Ameliah touches the top of the shell.

— Yeah.

— We moved around so much. She never took it off.

— I know.

She looks up at Nan.

— Do you believe in the universe? I mean, you know, forces and stuff.

Nan points at the shell with her toast.

— When stuff like that happens, I think it's hard not to, you know? They were so young, the pair of them, I mean, straight out of university, but when it's meant to be.

She stares into space as she takes a bite.

— That poor guy didn't stand a chance.

— Which guy?

Nan swallows.

— The one she was with at college, when your dad showed up.

She takes another bite. Ameliah thinks about Dad turning up at Mum's college, seeing the necklace, seeing her.

— It's funny, whenever Mum told the story, I always imagined violins playing or something, you know? Dramatic music, out of nowhere.

Nan smiles at her.

221

— Like a film.

— Yeah, like a film.

Nan lays her hand on top of Ameliah's, on top of the shell.

— Let's hope you get your own fairy tale, love.

Ameliah pictures the boy from the supermarket.

— Yeah.

Nan pushes the last of her toast into her mouth.

— Everybody wants a fairy tale.

Ryan stared at the screen of the arcade machine. He gripped the player-two joystick between the first two fingers of his upturned left hand, the fingertips of his right poised ready on the buttons. He could feel Nathan tensing up next to him, the pair of them waiting for the fight to begin.

— I haven't played in a while, just so you know.

Nathan's voice betrayed nerves that Ryan felt filling the muscles in his arms. The word flashed up on the screen as the machine called out 'Fight'.

Ameliah stares at the photograph. She turns the hardback book over in her hand to look at the cover. The dated lettering above the glossy photograph of what looks like a meteor shower spells the word COSMOS. She closes the book and looks back at the photo. Two boys stand next to each other, forcing smiles.

One of them is slightly taller. His hair is much fairer than the other boy and his smile is more sarcastic.

Ameliah stares at the shorter boy. His dark wiry hair. His open face. His baggy clothes can't hide his lean frame. Above them the lights of the shiny building glow multicoloured around the large red letters of the word AMUSEMENTS.

She turns the photograph over. Written in the top left-hand corner in blue biro are the words 'With Nathan, 1993'.

— Yes!

Ryan punches the air as his character connects with a triple-hit dragon punch, sending Nathan's sumo wrestler on to his back for the victory. Nathan slaps the machine next to the buttons.

— My buttons were sticking. I told you I haven't played for ages.

— Yeah, I can tell.

Ryan saw his reflection smiling in the screen as it flashed dark.

— Rematch.

Nathan fished in his pocket for more coins. Dad and Sophia came up behind them, carrying crisps and cans of drink.

— Who wants the Lilt?

Sophia held up the can like a hostess on a game show. Nathan grabbed for it. Sophia pulled it back out of his reach.

— Ryan, would you like the Lilt?

Ryan glanced at Nathan then shook his head.

— He can have it, it's fine.

Nathan smiled and took the can. Dad and Sophia stared at him. He looked at Ryan.

— Yeah, thanks.

— Right, well, this is going great, don't you think?

Dad stuck a thumb up and nodded his head.

— I reckon another three hours and we're there, if my lovely navigator stays on task.

He laid his hand on Sophia's shoulder. She cut him a stare.

— I'm just saying what the map says, Michael.

She handed Ryan a can of Pepsi. Nathan looked at Ryan and smiled. Dad took a deep breath.

— Let's hit the road, gang.

Ryan watched Dad and Sophia walk away towards the service station doors. He turned to Nathan. Nathan took a swig of his can then looked down.

— Can't you even tie your laces?

Ryan glanced at his shoes and felt the sting of pain as Nathan slapped him on the back of the neck. He looked up, rubbing his neck, and saw Nathan jogging backwards towards the exit smiling straight at him.

— Is that my dad?

Ameliah holds up the photograph in front of her. Nan leans into the spare room, holding on to the frame of the door.

— I can't see, love, you ready to go?

Ameliah points a finger at the shorter boy with the dark hair. Nan squints.

— I really can't see. It could be, pass it here.

Ameliah hands her the photograph. Nan stands up

straight, holding the photo in front of her.

— Yeah, I think that's your dad.

Nan nods uncertainly.

— I'm not sure who he's with though, must be a friend?

— Nathan.

Ameliah points at the photograph.

— It says, *with Nathan*. On the back.

— Oh.

Nan flips over the photograph.

— Where was it?

Ameliah looks at the book in her lap. She holds it up in two hands.

— It was in this, on its own between the pages.

Nan lowers the photo and looks down at the book.

— *Cosmos*, Carl Sagan. Well, if it's a science book, it makes sense that it's your dad. Are there any more?

Ameliah watches Nan looking at the boxes on the floor.

— Books?

— Photos.

— No. Not in the book anyway. There's probably more in some of the boxes. He looks so young. I never heard him mention anyone called Nathan.

Nan shakes her head and hands the photo back to Ameliah.

— No, you wouldn't.

Ameliah looks up at her.

— Why not?

— They fell out, and that was that. Families, eh?

— What do you mean?

Nan shrugs.

— I mean they're not easy, are they? Especially stepbrothers and sisters.

— What?

Ameliah's mouth hangs open. Nan looks at her.

— Nathan was your dad's stepbrother, when his dad remarried.

Ameliah felt her head spinning.

— What?!

Nan nodded.

— Yeah, I don't think the marriage lasted very long, I mean I'm not sure, I don't know the details. All I know is that the two boys fell out and didn't speak again.

Ameliah feels her words sticking to the inside of her throat.

— Dad had a brother?

Nan shakes her head.

— Stepbrother. Very different.

— And he never told me?

Nan sighs.

— I guess he didn't see the point. I mean they stopped speaking before you were born and I don't think he ever expected them to speak again. I think it was a pretty big fight.

Ameliah glances up at the ceiling then looks at Nan.

— About what?

Nan presses her lips together.

— About your mum.

She stares at the boxes against the wall. Ameliah looks at the photograph in her hand. The two boys stare out.

— I remember him saying there weren't any photos of him. From when he was a boy.

— Who?

— Your dad. I remember looking through an old album with him and your mum, not long after you were born, and he said that he used to refuse to be in photographs.

— Refuse?

— Yeah, he said he'd run off or get out of it somehow. He said he was pretty sure there wasn't a single photo of him through his whole teens. Don't ask me why I've just remembered that.

Ameliah looks up at Nan.

— Why did they fight about Mum?

Nan shrugs awkwardly. Ameliah looks back at the photograph. She stares at Dad and tries to imagine him talking as a boy.

— What else am I going to find out? Have I got a long-lost twin sister?

Nan smiles at her.

— Very funny, love. Nobody meant any harm — things get complicated as you get older. Grudges run deep sometimes. I used to have a best friend, we worked together in the bakery from when we were what, seventeen. Thick as thieves we were, then we fell out, over a boy I think, I can't even remember it's that long ago, and bam, we never spoke again.

Ameliah looks around her. The carpet is now half visible, with most of the boxes and bags stacked against the wall to the left. The room feels lighter now the window isn't blocked. She puffs out her cheeks.

— I'd say they were pretty complicated already.

Nan rubs her hands together.

— I thought we could get some popcorn. You like popcorn, right?

Ameliah opens the book and lays the photograph in the crease of the page. She pictures the two boys walking along a street, kicking a flattened can as they go. She stands up. Nan frowns.

— Don't be offended, sweetheart. Us grown-ups make choices, and they're not always the right ones.

Ameliah looks at Nan and thinks about her being left to pick up the pieces. Nan smiles and rubs her hand on Ameliah's shoulder.

— Salted or sweet?

Ameliah smiles.

— Whatever you like best, Nan.

Nan laughs.

— Do you really think I'm fussy?

CHAPTER 8

— I'm not singing.

Nathan shook his head in the rear-view mirror. Sophia rolled her eyes in the passenger seat. Ryan stared at the side of Dad's face as he drove along the motorway.

— No way.

Nathan looked at Ryan.

— Help me out, mate.

Ryan nodded.

— He's right. I've gotta say I'm with him on this one. I think maybe you two think we're seven or something.

— Exactly. You hear that, Michael? Mum?

Sophia looked at Dad.

— I think we're facing some kind of uprising.

She turned back to the two boys.

— This smells like mutiny.

Dad glanced across at her.

— There's only one thing to do with mutineers.

Nathan and Ryan groaned as Dad started to sing at the top of his voice.

— Oh, you never go to heaven!

Sophia's response was equally loud.

— Oh, you never go to heaven!

— In a biscuit tin!

— In a biscuit tin!

— Cos a biscuit tin!

Nathan banged the inside of his door.

— *Noooooooooooooooo!*

Sophia and Dad laughed as they carried on singing. Ryan looked at all three of them and felt himself smile.

The wall of DVDs stretches out in either direction. Nan screws up her face.

— I haven't got a clue, love, what do you fancy?

Ameliah stares at the covers on the New Releases shelf, not recognising anything.

— I dunno, Nan. This is hard work.

— I'll go next door and get the popcorn. They charge an arm and a leg in here and you only get a thimbleful. You find something and I'll meet you by the ice-cream fridge, right?

Ameliah nods. Nan walks away towards the exit. Ameliah turns round. The small speakers in the ceiling push out a cheesy instrumental. Shelves and shelves full of plastic cases all around her. She starts walking slowly down a short aisle, pointing a finger vaguely at titles as she goes. She remembers sitting in the cinema in between Mum and Dad, the curtains moving apart that extra bit, letting them know the feature film was about to start. Mum whispering through the film, asking questions and saying things like I don't trust him or she's definitely a baddie. Dad shushing them both and pointing seriously at the screen. Watching the light on their faces and how young they looked.

— Into the classics then?

Joe stands just on the other side of the shelves. His face is newly shaven, but his dirty-blond hair is still as scruffy. She can only see the top half of his body. She feels panic in her stomach as she looks past him towards the exit, trying to spot Nan.

233

Joe holds up a DVD and smiles.

— I'm a sucker for the eighties.

Ameliah looks at the cover. A young man stands raising his sunglasses from his shocked face, while behind him an older man in a white coat copies his expression under the block letters of *Back to the Future*.

— I've seen it.

Joe lowers the DVD and looks at the back.

— Great Scott! Classic. I even like the third one. Have you seen the third one?

Ameliah presses her feet into the threadbare shop carpet.

— Yeah. I watched them all with my dad.

Joe stares at the case in his hands. Ameliah looks towards the exit. The ceiling speakers start a new tune.

— Yeah. He did love 'em.

Ameliah looks at him. His light chocolate-coloured jacket obscures the red writing on his dark blue T-shirt. She thinks she sees part of the word Mars. Joe looks up.

— You on your own?

— I'm with my nan. She'll be back any minute.

Joe smiles.

— OK. Take it easy, I'm not some weirdo.

Ameliah looks at him. They stand in silence.

— I should go. I have to choose something.

She starts to walk away from him. He raises the DVD.

— OK. Yeah, well, enjoy your film, whatever you choose.

Ameliah feels him watching her back as she walks away. She still can't see Nan. She turns quickly and walks back towards him. His face is surprised.

— When did I meet you? she asks.

She can feel her hands hot next to her hips as she stares at him. He shuffles his feet slightly.

— You really don't remember?

He gazes at her, his head to one side. Ameliah can't work out how old he is.

— No.

She holds his stare, trying not to blink. He looks at the floor then back at her.

— Your mum's funeral.

He looks down again. Ameliah feels her chest get heavy. She remembers Dad standing up in front of everyone, trying to read from a piece of paper, his hands getting the better of him as everyone watched.

— You were what, nine then?

Ameliah looks at Joe, trying to place him at the funeral.

— Ten.

An overexcited voice speaks over the cheesy music from the speakers.

— This week only, choose three titles and pay for just two, that's three titles for the price of two.

He looks up at the ceiling.

— That's stupid, nobody ever gets through three films.

He shakes his head. Ameliah watches him.

— So you weren't at the accident?

He looks at her.

— What?

Ameliah checks herself quickly.

— Where in America?

She points a finger at him.

— Your accent, it's American.

His face doesn't change.

— North Carolina. Eleven years, more or less.

He points to his left.

— West.

He puffs out his cheeks.

— A lot more sun than here, I can tell ya.

He nods the nod of forced small talk.

— OK, so I think I've made my choice. I'll see you later, Ameliah. Say hi to your nan for me.

He walks away. Ameliah watches his back and knows he can feel her. As he approaches the exit, he places the DVD on to the nearest shelf and walks out through the glass doors.

Ameliah stares through the shop window into the fading light of the car park.

She thinks about Dad. Sitting with him on the sofa, watching him watch the film out of the corner of her eye, laughing when he laughed, wanting to share his fun.

— Haven't you picked yet?

Nan holds two large bags of popcorn and a tub of ice cream.

— Sorry I took so long, I couldn't choose. Do you like mint choc chip?

She smiles a hungry smile. Ameliah snaps out of her daydream and looks at Nan.

— Yeah, great. Did you just see?

— What, love?

Nan looks round.

— Nothing.

Ameliah looks at the shelf to her left. All the covers are for films made before she was born. She sees one showing a lady wearing a light pink dress in the arms of a man dressed all in black. *Dirty Dancing.* She picks it up.

— Got one.

Nan looks at the case and smiles.

— Old school. I like it.

A seagull squawked overhead. Ryan could hear the sound of the sea in the distance as he stared at the caravan.

Its metal support legs looked like a strong kick would break them. The bulky beige and brown cabin looked like it had been made by a baby out of empty cereal boxes.

All around it identical caravans were lined up in both directions, poorly lit by the weak strip light above each door.

He heard Sophia's laugh from inside and thought about turning round and walking away. The door swung open and Nathan jumped down the three chunky steps, wobbling slightly on the grass then steadying himself. Sophia's laugh got louder through the open door. He swung it shut, muting her cackle.

— This is bad.

He shook his head.

— It's like being in a cupboard. They're acting like kids.

Ryan looked at the caravan. The cream-coloured curtains made the window blend seamlessly with the outside wall.

— Let's leave 'em to it. There's an arcade down the other side.

Nathan nodded.

— Fine, I honestly thought I was gonna throw up. They could've left us at home.

As the pair of them walked between caravans, Ryan thought about Eve. He pictured the thin sliver of her body through the crack in the fence and the sound of her voice.

— What are you smiling for?

Nathan poked his arm. Ryan breathed deeply, filling his lungs with fresh air.

— Can you smell the sea?

— Sea? All I smell is seagull shit and fishermen's armpits.

Ryan laughed. Nathan looked at him, his face screwed up in disgust.

— I'm serious. I don't even know what this place is. Who comes here?

His face looked genuinely confused and Ryan couldn't help laughing again. Nathan's expression softened.

— It's not funny, man. Who knows what goes on here?

He tried to keep a serious face, but cracked as Ryan stared at him. They both laughed as they approached the front of a large building. Its big flashing red sign spelled AMUSEMENTS.

The lady in the pink dress runs towards the man in black as the song builds to a chorus. She jumps, he lifts her above her head, her arms stretched out like a plane, as all around them people kick over chairs and dance.

Ameliah feels the muscles in her cheeks as she lets out a warm sigh, holding her hand to her chest. She thinks about this being Mum's kind of film, how she can imagine Mum teary-eyed at the end of it, a big smile across her face, gripping Dad's arm as they sit on the sofa on a Friday night.

She looks across at Nan. She's fast asleep, head tilted back, mouth wide open as she snores.

As the end credits start to roll, Ameliah stares at the

TV and thinks about Joe. Why was he at the DVD shop? Did he know she followed him?

She tries to picture him and Dad together, sitting at a table laughing, but it just feels like putting two different photographs together that don't belong.

Was it the funeral she remembered him from?

She feels the start of a headache as the TV screen goes darker and is suddenly aware of how late it must be. She looks at Nan and decides it's probably best to leave her there rather than wake her up.

Why can't she remember him? What does he want?

She feels her brain pressing the inside of her skull as she switches off the TV. Nan stirs, like a farm animal having a dream. Ameliah smiles in the dark and walks towards the kitchen.

Standing at the sink, she stares at her reflection in the dark window. Her high cheekbones cast small shadows either side of her full lips. She drags her curls back over her head with the palm of her hand and tilts her chin slightly to get a better look at her eyes and forehead.

The shadows make her face look like a mask, one of those tribal masks with diamond-shaped eyes cut out of wood, and it strikes her that she looks like Mum.

Throwing the two pills in her mouth, she gulps water from a glass and breathes deeply, hoping that the paracetamol will kick in immediately.

— You OK, love?

Nan's voice is heavy with tired as she stands in the doorway. Ameliah stares at her reflection, feeling the pulse of blood behind her eyes.

— I'm fine. Just a headache.

Nan turns her head, cracking her neck.

— Time for bed, don't you think?

Ameliah nods. Nan smiles.

— You know sometimes I look at you and it's like a time warp or something.

She shakes her head slowly. Ameliah looks at her.

— What was she like, Nan, I mean when she was my age?

Nan closes her mouth and breathes deeply through her nose.

— She was tough.

Ameliah watches Nan remembering.

— Am I like her?

Nan looks at her and smiles.

— Sweetheart, the apple never falls far from the tree.

Nan walks towards her.

— My mother used to say there's fire in our blood and it takes a lifetime to tame it.

She presses her hand against the side of Ameliah's face. Ameliah feels the heat against her skin and presses her cheek into Nan's hand.

— Why would it happen, Nan? How is it fair?

Nan lowers her head so their eyes are level.

— Sweetheart, most people don't even get half a day of what your mum and dad had with each other. It's hard for us left behind, but maybe they just had to be together.

Ameliah feels her lungs against the inside of her chest. She gets a flash of Mum sticking her tongue out at her from the school gate, lined up with the other mums at the fenced entrance, the others waving seriously, Mum blowing raspberries, her dark hair blowing in the wind. She remembers Mum whispering in her ear as she hugged her goodbye.

— Be good, and never be afraid to ask.

She feels her eyes welling up. Nan strokes the side of her head.

— She would be so proud of you.

She leans in and kisses Ameliah on the forehead then straightens up.

— Come on, I think it's time to sleep. We'll go together in the morning, say happy birthday.

She strokes Ameliah's hair. Ameliah looks up at her

— I'm sorry for what I said, about Richard.

Nan nods and steps towards the door.

— I know you are, love. Don't worry about it.

— Do you like him?

Ameliah watches Nan lean against the door frame.

— Yeah, I think I do.

— You should tell him.

Nan smiles.

— I see. Is that what you do?

Ameliah thinks about the supermarket boy and feels the blood in her cheeks. Nan bites her bottom lip.

— Who is he?

Ameliah shrugs and looks away.

— I don't know.

Nan's smile widens.

— Well, when you get to my age, it's a little more complicated. You can't just dive in, you know? You need to test the water a bit first, before you're ready. You know what I mean?

Ameliah shrugs. Nan pushes off the door frame and stands up straight.

— The waters change. And once you jump in, it's harder to get out, you know?

Ameliah looks at her.

— So it's like swimming?

— Yeah, in a manner of speaking, and maybe you haven't been swimming in a while, so you have to be ready. You have to be ready to jump in.

Nan stares into space as though trying to listen to herself. Ameliah can hear the hum of the fridge. Nan looks at her.

— But I guess you can't just stand there on the side forever either, can you? You need to move on, right?

She smiles.

— Listen to me, I'm talking to myself now. Come on, you, time to sleep.

Ameliah smiles back and wonders what the boy is doing right now.

The caravan was quiet. Ryan stared at the electric blue numbers on the microwave display as he lay on the thin cushion of the sofa bed. He could feel the wooden edge of the seat digging into his spine, like he was balancing on the edge of a cliff. The flimsy blinds didn't really block much of the strip light from outside.

He looked down his sleeping bag to where his feet reached the corner of the L-shaped seating. The bottom of Nathan's sleeping bag was just a couple of inches away from his and he pictured them from above looking like three o'clock. He thought about Eve, leaning over him as he lay on the long grass of her nan's back lawn. How it felt like he was telling her things without opening his mouth. How he wanted to do something big—

— Don't touch me.

Nathan's whisper was angry. He tried to shuffle himself further along the sofa, moving his feet away from Ryan's, but nearly slid off the narrow seat. He grabbed the back cushions just in time to stop himself. Ryan giggled.

— Shut up. This is a joke.

Ryan tried to see Nathan's face through the legs of the cheap breakfast bar in between them.

— How the hell are you supposed to sleep on the edge of a knife? How come they get the bed?

Nathan's voice forgot to whisper. Ryan imagined sharing a bed with Nathan and suddenly felt a lot more comfortable where he was.

— It's not that bad.

He heard the angry rustle of Nathan's sleeping bag.

— Shut up, Ryan. Not that bad? You don't always have to play the angel, you know.

— Angel?

Nathan mocked his voice.

— It's not that bad, ooh, yes please, Sophia, you're right, Dad, can I help you with that?

— What? Shut up!

— A caravan holiday, oh whoopee! Does anyone need me to lick their bum?

— Shut your mouth, Nathan! You think I want to be here? With you, and them, in there?

Nathan didn't answer. Ryan sat up, his body and arms still inside his sleeping bag.

— If you weren't always such a knob, we wouldn't even be here.

Nathan sat up and stared at Ryan. Ryan stared back, his eyes trying to focus.

— It's all your shit that's making them think we need to 'bond' or whatever, so don't have a go at me like I've done something wrong.

— What did you call me?

Nathan lifted his arms out of his sleeping bag. Ryan looked down.

— Did you call me a knob?

Ryan lay back down on his side, pulling his sleeping back up higher around his neck.

— Get lost, Nathan, just go to sleep.

Nathan nodded aggressively.

— Yeah, I thought so. Lie down, baby.

Ryan felt his stomach tighten as Nathan lay back down. He stared at the cheap carpet, the dark swirls matted like little dreadlocks, and imagined waking up to the aftermath of a hurricane, Nathan's side of the caravan completely destroyed.

CHAPTER 9

Nan turns the car out of the cemetery on to the dual carriageway. Ameliah stares out of the passenger window at the semi-detached houses. Nan folds down her sun visor as light streams in through the windscreen. She lets out a heavy sigh. Ameliah looks across at her, her cheeks still flushed from crying.

She thinks about Mum's funeral. Strangers standing silently, waiting for someone to tell them they could breathe out. She remembers Nan staring down at the ground, her eyes dry, like she was too angry to cry.

— She would've been thirty-four, I mean how's that—

Nan stares ahead as she speaks. The car approaches an island. Ameliah tries to picture what a thirty-four-year-old woman looks like, but all she sees is Nan's face, staring down at the ground.

249

She thinks about the graves, side by side like grey stone twins. The small squares of marble where the flowers go. Her mind moves in closer, down to the dirt, through the soil, layers of dark and worms to the coffins and—

— Idiot!

Ameliah is thrown forward and feels her seat belt dig into her chest as Nan slams on the brakes. A large silver saloon car moves past, the driver shaking his middle-aged head at them.

— Oh, get lost! I've got right of way, you idiot!

She sticks up two fingers. Ameliah is shocked, but before she knows what she's doing her fingers are up too, backing Nan up in their angry salute. Nan glances at her and nods. The driver looks away as the saloon car pulls off. Nan holds her pose, her breathing ragged.

Ameliah looks at their hands next to each other, old and young, and thinks of those posters showing the evolution of man. Mum's hand the missing link between their two.

Nan lowers her hand and looks at Ameliah.

— I'm sorry, love. Some people.

Ameliah lowers hers and feels her fingers relax.

— It's OK, Nan, he looked like an idiot.

A car beeps behind them. Ameliah knows they are both fighting the same image in their heads. The crumpled car wreck. The blue lights. Nan takes the wheel.

— He really did, didn't he?

Ameliah nods. Nan smiles as they drive round the roundabout.

— I don't know about you, but I could eat.

Ameliah remembers after the funeral, people back at the house eating small bits of food on paper plates. Old relatives she'd never met sitting in little horseshoes of chairs, silently shaking their heads as she moved between them. Nan cleaning up after people before they'd really finished. A couple of older men with red faces holding thick glasses half full of dark liquid. Dad at the back door in his dark suit talking to someone.

Walking through the kitchen towards him. His body gets more animated, his hands gesturing in front of him as though he's arguing a point. His body blocks the doorway as she taps him on the back. Dad turns to her, his face angry. His expression softens as he sees her, he leans forward and she can see past him, out on to the small garden patio, and there his is, wearing a brown suit that's too small for him, holding a rolled cigarette, looking at Dad.

Joe.

His face screwed up under his rough nest of dirty-blond hair.

Ryan dug at the damp sand with his fingers like a shovel, scraping a small trench next to his crossed legs. The perfect white shell sat on his thigh like a miniature Japanese fan. Nathan stood at the edge of the water a stone's throw in front of him, shot-putting rocks into the murky sea.

The beach was mostly empty. Scattered families role playing like they were on the French Riviera, huddled against stripy windbreaks. Behind them, the jagged wall of the cliffs stood solid as, high above, seagulls circled, waiting for someone to drop a sandwich.

Ryan thought about breakfast earlier, Dad and Sophia giggling like teenagers as they all ate Dad's car-crash omelette. Dad and Sophia telling him and Nathan to spend time together, him and Nathan rolling their eyes in unison, nodding begrudgingly.

Now here they were on the beach, both of them keeping their distance.

Ryan watched water collect in the bottom of his little trench and thought about the scene from *Star Wars* when they get trapped in the garbage disposal on the Death Star. He pushed the sand on either side of the trench with his hands, making the walls cave in.

— Come in, 3PO!

A shoe-sized rock hit the sand inches from his knee. He looked up and was about to go mad when he saw Nathan's expression.

— Those kids are here.

He nodded to his left, keeping his eyes on Ryan. Ryan turned his head.

— Don't look, you idiot.

— What kids?

— Them older ones, from the arcade. I told you.

— You didn't tell me anything.

— Whatever, they were giving me grief.

Ryan noticed Nathan was holding a tennis-ball-sized rock in his right hand.

— What's that for?

— Don't worry about that. Stand up.

Ryan felt a stab of nerves as he lifted himself on to his feet.

— Act like you're talking to me.

Nathan exaggerated a nod, faking conversation. Ryan could feel him pumping himself up.

— What's going on, Nath?

Nathan's eyes narrowed.

— The one kid, the big one, he seemed like the hardest. Just stay calm.

Ryan wondered whether Nathan was talking to him or himself. He felt out of his depth as Nathan turned to face the group of boys making their way over. Ryan turned too, standing next to Nathan, feeling the muscles in his arms tense.

There were four of them, all dressed in versions of the same ripped jeans, dark T-shirt or checked shirt outfit. All of them had hair to their shoulders. All of them were bigger than Ryan. He figured they must be eighteen, seventeen at least. The one leading was as big as Liam. Ryan wished his best friend was with them now.

— We should run.

He glanced at Nathan. Nathan dug his heels in the sand.

— If you run, I'll hit you myself.

He stared at the boys.

— Just do what I do, all right?

Ryan tried to puff up his chest as the boys stopped a

table-width away, curving round them like a boomerang. He noticed a couple of them had stubble on their chins. He made out Nirvana album T-shirts on at least three of them.

— You in the arcade again last night?

The big one spoke like he thought he was in a film. Ryan decided it was best not to point that out. Nathan stared straight at the boy.

— Yeah, we were, so what?

The two boys furthest to the left looked at each other and smiled. Ryan could taste his breakfast in his throat.

— Which one of you is Ryu?

Ryan gulped as he remembered the night before, playing the Out Run machine in the arcade and completing the game. He had tried to enter his name, but accidentally pressed 'u' from the letters board. He hadn't told Nathan because he knew he'd give him grief about thinking he was a Street Fighter character.

The boys all stood waiting. The big one stared at Nathan. Nathan looked at Ryan like that wasn't what he was expecting them to say. Ryan opened his mouth to tell Nathan, but before he could speak Nathan turned back to the boys.

— I am.

Ryan watched Nathan as he stepped forward. The big kid

stepped forward too and squared up to Nathan while the others bunched together behind him.

— What kind of name is Ryu?

Nathan didn't wobble.

— It's my kind of name.

The boy was nearly a head taller than Nathan and half an extra body wide, but Nathan didn't seem scared.

— Why do you care?

The boy lifted his shoulders, like he was getting ready to bench-press a caravan. The boy on the right with greasy black hair chipped in.

— He cares cos you beat his top score.

The big boy cut his friend a glance; his friend looked down. Nathan glanced back at Ryan. Ryan shrugged. Nathan turned back to the boy.

— On what?

The big boy looked confused.

— What do mean on what? Out Run.

Nathan shrugged.

— Well, I'm sorry, mate, I can't help it if I'm good at the game.

— Knock him out, Deano!

The boy's voice was higher than the others, like a car's screeching wheels. Ryan looked at him, standing behind the big one, his pale face egging his friend on. Ryan imagined a long lizard tongue shooting out of the boy's mouth as he spoke.

— Go on, Dean, he's well cocky.

Their accents sounded strange, like they were stretching words out for no reason.

Ryan felt panic course through him. He thought about running. There were other people on the beach — Nathan wouldn't get beaten up too badly before somebody stopped it.

Deano planted himself. Ryan watched Nathan's hand squeeze the rock, his knuckles empty of blood from the tightness of his grip. This wasn't going to end well—

— We should compete, I mean you two should compete, on the game, that's the only way to know who's best.

Everyone looked at him. Ryan felt himself shrink a little bit.

— It makes sense, right? If you want your top score back, just play him. You can even play other games, like a tournament.

He felt everyone's eyes narrow.

— A tournament?

The boy with greasy hair seemed to not know what the word meant. His head moved like it was trying to snake away from his shoulders. Ryan clarified.

— A competition. They both play a bunch of games and the winner is the one with the highest scores.

— What are you talking about?

The spotty boy on the far left stared at him.

— That's stupid. Just deck him, Deano.

The others grunted their agreement like a pack of apes. Nathan looked at Ryan like he was just seeing him for the first time. Ryan felt the twist in his gut of a bad idea. He saw Deano pull his arm back as Nathan turned back to face him.

— Nath!

Nathan's body folded in half as the punch hit his stomach. He fell to his knees as all the air left his body. Deano stood over him with clenched fists. Ryan ran to Nathan, dropping to the ground next to him. Nathan's eyes were closed in pain.

— You OK? What do I do?

Nathan opened his eyes, his face flushed red, his mouth gasping for air. Deano's voice sounded louder from above them.

— Let's go. This midget's not worth breaking a sweat.

He turned to go. The others followed, mirroring his turn like foot soldiers.

Ryan put his hand across Nathan's shoulders. Nathan coughed and shrugged him off.

— Get off me.

— Can you breathe?

— Of course I can breathe, you idiot, he caught me with a cheap shot.

He lifted himself to his feet, leaning with his hands on his knees, and spat on to the sand.

— I can't believe you stood up to him. They must've been at least eighteen, d'you reckon?

Nathan stood up and tested his lungs before wheezing and bending over again.

— Nath? Seriously, you got some balls, man.

Nathan looked at him.

— Tournament?

Ryan looked down.

— I dunno, I was trying to distract 'em, stop us getting a kicking.

— Tournament?

— OK, OK, it was stupid, I'm sorry.

Nathan stood up again. Along the beach the older boys looked like small Warhammer figures.

— Since when did you get top score on Out Run?

Nathan stared at him. Ryan shrugged.

— And Ryu? Why would you do that?

— It was a mistake. The joystick slipped.

— You're such a weirdo, Ryan.

Nathan started to walk away. Ryan followed him.

— No I'm not. Look, thanks. For standing up for me and that.

Nathan looked at him, holding his ribs as they walked.

— I wasn't standing up for you, he was a dick. Sometimes you just have to jump in.

Ryan smiled. Nathan frowned.

— Don't start getting all bummy on me again.

— Sorry. Come on, I'll get us a hot dog from that stall place. I've got two quid.

Nathan looked at him and shook his head.

— I want chips with it.

Ameliah stares at the small metal box attached to the wall. Two square buttons show the house is split into two flats. The card next to the bottom button reads 'Roberts'. The top button's card has been taken out. Ameliah stares at the plastic rectangle where the name should be.

She digs her hands into the pockets of Heather's thin blue hoody, noticing how similar its colour is to the front door, and feels happy she chose to wear it. A bus moves past on the street behind her. She turns, watching the airbrushed woman on its large side advert smile as she floats along.

Ameliah pulls out her phone and looks at the screen. She pushes the select button with her thumb to open the new message. Her lips mouth the words as she reads.

— Film starts 1.30. Ring me straight after OK? Hx

She puts her finger on the top button and pushes. There's no sound. She steps back, looking up at the upper bay window. The net curtains are gone and through the glass she can see the end of an empty bookshelf high on one wall.

She presses the button again, keeping her eyes on the window, looking for any signs that he's in. She steps forward to knock on the door just as it opens.

Joe is wearing a dark green dressing gown. His hair is even messier than usual. Ameliah looks down at his hairy calves and long feet. She feels a wave of embarrassment wash over her.

— Sorry. Sorry, I didn't mean to wake you up.

Joe rubs his eyes with the palms of his hands then stretches his mouth and face.

— No. It's fine. Bit of a surprise but fine.

He rolls his neck to either side and yawns.

— I should go, this is a bad time.

Ameliah steps back. Joe sniffs and shakes his head.

— No, I mean don't go. Does your nan know you're here?

His voice sounds like he's reading from a script. Ameliah shakes her head then looks over her shoulder along the road. A string of cars wait at the traffic lights.

— Come in.

He steps aside as she walks past him then leans out and looks both ways before closing the door.

The room is bigger than she'd imagined. The exposed floorboards have been stained deep brown. Boxes and bags are everywhere and Ameliah pictures the spare room at Nan's house.

A high empty bookshelf runs along the full length of the wall to the right. Halfway along the wall a deep bookcase holds large academic-looking books and stacks of vinyl records. Next to the bookcase an old dark wooden table is folded into a semi-circle and Ameliah can see a turntable, two different stereos and a machine that looks like a large cassette tape with no edges. She thinks about the old cassette player back on her bedside table as she notices tapes and CDs stacked and scattered on the table and the floor.

Joe sticks his head round the door behind her.

— I'm just gonna jump in the shower. Have a seat if you like.

He looks round the room.

— Sorry about the mess, not properly moved in yet, all a bit of a rush. I can't find the remote, but the telly works.

He points to a large flat-screen in the far corner on a low cabinet. Ameliah nods.

Joe disappears. She steps into the room, taking care not to tread on anything. She sees two large sports bags full of clothes on the floor in front of an old fireplace and a set of dumb-bells with heavy weights on each end. DVDs and books are stacked in small piles like Stonehenge.

Her eyes are drawn back to the table with the tapes.

She sits down on the low battered leather sofa and feels herself sink into it. The sound of the shower kicks in from down the hall and for a second she panics and thinks about leaving.

— What are you doing?

She stares at her reflection in the dark matt screen of the TV, watching her mouth speak the words. To her left, through the window, she can see the tops of cars moving past. Across the street the houses look further away than they did from the pavement.

She thinks she hears Joe singing, his muffled voice moving up and down, and for a second she pictures his face, his hair darker from the water and flat against his head, his dark eyes. She shakes her head and pulls a face.

— Seriously, what are you doing?

She reaches for the memory of Mum's funeral. Dad's dark suit, looking past him out through the kitchen door, Joe standing there, his face torn between angry and confused—

— That's better.

He walks in barefoot, wearing light jeans and a white T-shirt clearly often washed with darks. He rubs his wet hair with a small lime-green towel.

— It's a bit of a bomb site, right? It always surprises me how much crap I've actually got.

He looks at her sharply.

— Sorry, I mean stuff.

Ameliah looks up at him.

— I'm thirteen, Joe, I can handle crap.

Joe smiles.

— Yeah, course, sorry.

— How old are you?

Joe looks at her, taken back. Ameliah shrugs

— I'm just curious. I mean you dress funny.

Joe looks down at himself.

— Funny?

— You know, young.

He looks at his feet then at her.

— How old do you think I am?

Ameliah's eyes narrow as she looks him up and down. Joe stands up straight.

— Come on, don't hold back.

He holds his arms out straight. Ameliah shakes her head.

— I dunno. Forget it.

She looks over at the old table. Joe follows her eyes.

— Why are you here?

Ameliah feels the stab of nerves in her chest. She looks at him sheepishly. He shakes his head.

— That came out wrong, sorry. What I meant was, I mean, I'm glad you came.

— I remembered you.

His face turns serious. She pictures him in a brown suit, too small for his body.

— I saw you at the funeral. You were outside, by the back door, with my dad.

Joe shifts his weight nervously.

— What did you see?

He looks at her and for a second she can see his face much younger, a boy waiting to be told off.

— You were wearing a brown suit.

Joe smiles nervously.

— Yeah.

— It didn't fit.

— It was a friend's. I still don't have one.

— Were you and Dad arguing?

Joe's eyes shift, looking round the room. He rubs the back of his neck with the towel.

— What did you hear?

Ameliah shakes her head.

— Nothing.

— Nothing?

— No. I can't remember.

Joe stares at her.

— You look so much like her.

Outside the window, a grey articulated lorry waits at the traffic lights. Ameliah looks out at its panelled trailer. She touches the side of her face.

— Yeah.

The lorry lets out a blast of air as its wheels roll into life again. Ameliah jumps as the towel hits the sofa next to her. Joe claps his hands together.

— What music you into?

His body springs into action like he got an electric shock. He rubs his hands together as he moves to the old table. Ameliah tries to think. Joe looks back at her, his eyes dancing.

— Well?

Ameliah shrugs. He narrows his eyes.

— Come on, it's a pretty straightforward question, anything. Gimme a song.

He starts to rifle through tapes, knocking cases on to the floor in his excitement. Ameliah thinks about Mum's tapes.

— Nirvana?

Joe freezes. He looks at her.

— Nirvana?

His face is serious. Ameliah shrugs again.

— My mum liked them. I found some of her old tapes.

Joe stares at the tapes on the table. Ameliah leans forward.

— Did you know my mum?

He looks at her.

— Yeah. I did.

He slots a cassette into the older-looking silver stereo, presses play and starts rummaging through bags, looking for something. The sound starts and Ameliah is suddenly aware of speakers behind her in the corner, to her left next to the TV, as well as more over by the table. She wonders why someone would set up their sound system before unpacking their clothes. She pictures the spare room back at Nan's, the boxes and bags, as what sounds like a heartbeat comes out from the speakers.

— What's funny?

Joe hops backwards and sits down on a black beanbag, pulling on a dark grey sock.

Ameliah feels the sound vibrating up through her feet and realises that she's smiling. She straightens her face.

— Nothing.

She stares at the tall dark speaker next to the TV, hearing what sounds like people going over the edge of a roller coaster. The screams cut into drums and a low guitar. Joe smiles and sighs.

— Perfect. Man, this album got me through a lot.

Ameliah watches him roll back into the beanbag, kicking his feet into the air. She notices that his socks are odd. One dark grey, one white.

— What is it?

She looks back at the speaker. Joe rocks forward.

— Pink Floyd. *Dark Side of The Moon*. My old man used to love it.

— Who's Pink Floyd?

Joe looks at her.

— They're a band, I mean they were a band. Pioneers.

He closes his eyes, listening to the music. Ameliah stares at a small stack of DVDs.

— You don't like it?

Ameliah shrugs. Joe nods.

— Course. It is pretty old. I mean I couldn't stand it when I was your age. I got lots of other stuff.

He stands up and moves to the old table. Ameliah

reads the name John Wayne on the spine of one of the DVDs.

— My nan loves him.

— What's that?

Joe ejects the tape and the music cuts off.

— My nan, John Wayne, she loves him. We watched one of his films the other night cos I'd never seen one.

— What?

He looks confused.

— Are you kidding?

— Not you as well.

She rolls her eyes and leans back into the sofa.

— But he's John Wayne, although his real name was Marilyn, or Mavis or something.

Joe holds up an old record sleeve, inspecting it like a precious coin.

— Ah, Busta.

He eases out the black vinyl circle and spins it over with his palms, lowering it down on to the turntable. Ameliah hears the crackle from the speakers and thinks about the tape with the voice. The kick and snare jump out of the speakers and Ameliah feels the thump of the bass in her chest. She looks at Joe, now nodding his head with his eyes closed.

He mouths along as the deep voice roars the opening syllables.

Ameliah smiles as she recognises the song. She remembers it blasting from the stereo downstairs, loud enough for Dad to hear it while he washed the dishes. She feels warm.

— More like it for ya?

Joe bounces over, moving past her to the window, staring out.

Ameliah remembers Dad coming towards her, his arms stretched out in front of him, his hands covered in bubbles as he pretended to attack her in time to the beat.

— Woohah!

She feels her head itching to nod and remembers Dad's face, his bubble beard wobbling as he pulled a monster face.

— Don't fight it, Am! Woohah!

Joe looks nervously towards the speaker as the man's

voice says a word Ameliah doesn't remember being in the song. Joe glances at her.

— Whoops. Dirty version.

He jogs back to the turntable and cuts it off.

— I'm not doing very well, am I?

Ameliah feels the phone vibrate in her pocket. Joe slides the record back into its sleeve.

— Are you hungry?

Ameliah shakes her head as she clicks open the message.

— I'm fine thanks.

She reads Heather's words.

— Hows it goin? Hx

Joe looks round the room.

— Yeah, it's gonna take me a while to get this place nice.

— Why America?

Joe looks at her.

— You mean why was I there?

— Yeah.

— University. At first. Then my doctorate, then work, then, well, I just stayed.

— Aren't you married?

Joe's face hardens, then he smiles.

— Jeez, you don't hold back, do you?

Ameliah bites her bottom lip.

— Sorry.

— It's fine.

He looks down at his hands.

— No, I'm not married. Came close but, you know, I'm, let's say my people skills still need a bit of work.

— What do you do?

Ameliah looks up at him. Joe looks back, straightening the back of his hair with his palm.

— I'm a scientist, like your dad.

— What kind of science?

— Erm, it's physics basically.

— Mechanics?

Joe looks at her, his eyes wide.

— You know about mechanics?

Ameliah shakes her head.

— Not really, I just saw books.

Joe nods.

— My field is nanoscience really.

Ameliah's eyes narrow.

— What's that?

Joe holds up his hand, squeezing the tip of his thumb and index finger together.

— Really, really, really small stuff.

— And you're a professor?

Joe breathes out.

— Yeah, but I don't teach. I'm pretty much completely research. Hence, no suit.

He smiles and wrinkles his nose.

— Besides, like I said, my people skills. I've never really been a people person, you know?

He stares into space. Ameliah slips the phone back into her pocket.

— Yeah. Did you know his brother?

Joe's face freezes. Ameliah sits up.

— Stepbrother I mean. Nathan.

Joe looks down.

— Yeah, I knew him.

— What was he like?

Joe stares, like he's receiving messages from a hidden earpiece.

— Look, Ameliah...

Ameliah feels the phone vibrating in her pocket again. Joe carries on.

— See the thing is, about your dad...

The phone carries on buzzing. Ameliah takes it out and sees Heather's name. She smiles awkwardly.

— Sorry, it's my friend, I just need to answer. Hello.

Joe stares into space as she speaks to Heather.

— Yeah, not long. I'm leaving in a sec. I'll be there, OK, OK, bye.

She ends the call.

— Sorry. I should go, we're watching a film. What were you going to say?

Joe breathes deeply.

— Yeah, course. No problem, don't worry, there's plenty of time. You sure you don't want something to eat? I think there might be some cold pizza in the fridge.

Ameliah stands up.

— No thanks.

She moves towards the door. Joe goes to the table and starts to rummage around.

— See you later, Joe.

The words feel awkward coming out of her mouth and she regrets saying them.

— Wait! You wanna hear something cool?

He turns to her, holding out a tape, his face excited.

Ameliah reads the words 'Hip Hop' in thick black felt tip inside the bright orange zigzags of an explosion.

— Your dad made it for me before college.

He opens the cassette box and slides out the tape, handing her the case. Ameliah watches him move back to the stereo. She holds the empty case tightly in two hands, biting her lip. Joe presses fast forward and the sound of the whirring tape kicks in. Ameliah watches the back of his head shake as he watches the stereo.

— He was trying to get me into hip hop. I didn't like it at first, can you believe that? He made tapes all the time. He even had a tape journal.

— Journal?

Ameliah looks at the cassette sleeve through the plastic; the explosion has layers of yellow and red and obviously took some time to colour in. Joe clicks stop on the tape and turns to her.

— Yeah, like his thoughts and stuff. I think it started as a way to get over his mum.

He presses play and warm drums kick out from the speakers. Ameliah pictures younger Dad in the photograph from the spare room as the drums start to fade out. She looks at Joe.

— What is it?

Joe holds up a finger.

— Wait, it's coming.

The song finishes and the speakers hum with the sound of recorded silence. Ameliah smiles at how warm the sound of old things makes her feel then—

— Hello?

She stares at the speaker. The hum of the tape.

— Hello? Is this thing even still working?

It's a boy's voice, a bit older than her. She feels her heart beating as she looks at Joe. Joe smiles. The voice carries on.

— It's me. I guess you've listened to the whole tape now. I mean if you got this far and you're hearing me then you must have, stupid. Man, I can't believe this thing still works. What you think? You feeling it?

Ameliah shuffles up, getting closer to the speaker, her skin tingling.

— I hope so. In fact, you know what? If you're not into it, there must be something wrong with you cos that's basically the best hip-hop collection I've ever heard, every track is wicked. How much time have I got before it cuts off?

277

Ameliah holds her breath as she listens.

— I can't see it. Anyway, if you don't like it you can always give it to someone and say you made it, that's probably what you're gonna do anyway.

Ameliah feels a word move up along her throat.

— Dad?

She feels Joe standing next to her as the voice sighs.

— So that's it. Your hip hop collection 1997. No need to thank me, I know you won't. With any luck you won't even find this till you're unpacking. Take it easy, and I'll see you when I come visit.

The hum of silence rolls out then the play button snaps up as the tape ends. Ameliah stares at the speaker, feeling her nose twitch as her eyes fill with tears. She feels Joe's shoulder against hers.

— Pretty crazy, right?

He blows air from his mouth.

— He was nearly eighteen when he made that. We both were.

Ameliah looks up at Joe and sees him deep in thought. She wipes her eyes with the back of her sleeve.

— So you were close?

Joe looks at her.

— Yeah, kind of.

He nods a smile.

— I can make you a copy if you like, give it to you next time?

Ameliah gets a flash of lying on her bed in the old house, Dad lying on his back next to her, reading aloud from his old *Book of the Unexplained*.

— Yeah. Please.

She can still hear the voice in her head. She tries to picture Dad younger, but older than she is now. Joe rests his hand on her shoulder.

— We've got lots to talk about.

He smiles and Ameliah feels surprised that she's happy his hand is on her. This man she doesn't really know, who's a link to Dad, and then it hits her. The voice. It isn't just familiar because it's Dad, she's heard it before, through older speakers.

— I've gotta go.

She turns towards the door. Joe moves his hand.

— Oh, OK, yeah, course you do. Your friend, right?

Ameliah looks up at him, her mind dancing with her realisation.

— What? No, I mean yeah. Bye, Joe.

She reaches the door then turns back.

— And thanks.

Joe stands there.

— No problem. Listen, I was thinking that maybe you'd like to come over one night, for food or something? We could watch a John Wayne, you know? You could bring your nan too?

His face is hopeful. Ameliah smiles.

— Yeah. That sounds nice.

The American-style restaurant bustled with the early afternoon rush. Waiters and waitresses wore 1950s-style outfits with red and white striped shirts and white rectangle hats at an angle on their heads.

Ryan stared at his milkshake and felt the smooth shell in his pocket with his thumb. He pictured Eve, smiling as she looked at it. Nathan slurped his chocolate shake loudly. Sophia shook her head as she watched him. Dad smiled at the large burger in his hands.

— Hello, beautiful.

Sophia smiled at Dad as they looked at each other.

She ran her finger down the list of songs in the jukebox menu against the wall.

— Oh, they've got The Bangles. Mike, have you got change?

Dad closed his eyes as he sunk his teeth into his burger.

Nathan dug his fingers into his glass, wiping the chocolate ice cream from the sides. Ryan looked towards the kitchen as a waiter with a heavy rectangular body turned round. He felt his stomach drop as he recognised Deano from the beach. He ducked his head down.

— What are you doing?

Nathan licked his fingers. Ryan kept his hand low and pointed towards the kitchen. Nathan turned round. Ryan saw his chest deflate as he spotted Deano. Nathan turned back to him.

— What's he doing here?

Ryan stayed low.

— He must work here. What do we do?

Nathan's left eye twitched.

— Nothing.

— What do you do about what? What are you two up to?

Sophia looked at them both.

— Who are you hiding from, Ryan?

Ryan felt Nathan kick him in the shins.

— Yeah, Ryan, get up, man.

Ryan looked over at Deano as he carried a tray stacked with baskets of food, his thick shoulders stretching the stripes of his shirt. Sophia followed his eyes.

— Do you two know that boy?

Ryan looked down. Nathan rolled his eyes.

— Have you been making friends?

She smiled at Dad.

— I think our boys have been making friends with the locals.

Dad laid his burger back on to his plate and looked across the restaurant.

— He's a big lad, isn't he? How old is he? Did you guys meet in the arcade?

— We don't know him.

Nathan's voice is stern. He looks at Ryan.

— Do we, Ryan?

Ryan sits up.

— No, we don't. Who are we looking at?

Dad stuck out his arm.

— Him there, the big lad.

Ryan batted it down.

— What are you doing, Ryan?

— Don't point, Dad! I mean it's rude to point, right?

Sophia stared at him. Dad leaned forward, his elbows on the table.

— What's going on?

Ryan looked at Nathan. Nathan's eyes said no.

Ryan looked back at Dad.

— Nothing.

Dad's eyes narrowed.

— Did that boy give you trouble, Ryan?

Ryan glanced at Nathan. Dad followed his eyes.

— He gave you trouble, Nath?

Nathan looked at Dad.

— Nah, not me, not at all.

Dad smiled a controlled smile.

— What did he do? You can tell me, Nathan.

Nathan looked at Sophia.

— He didn't do anything. Mum, tell him.

Sophia looked at Dad then back at Nathan.

— Tell Michael what he did, Nathan.

Nathan rubbed his face with his hands.

— He hit him. On the beach. In the stomach.

Ryan felt the words jump out of his mouth. Nathan stared at him.

283

— Good one, squealer.

— He hit you? Nathan? Did that boy hit you?

Sophia leaned forward. Dad's face changed.

— He looks at least eighteen. When did he hit you?

— I dunno.

Nathan shook his head. Ryan looked at Dad.

— It was the day before yesterday, on the beach.

Nathan glared at Ryan. Dad stood up. Everyone looked at him.

— What are you doing, Michael?

Sophia seemed confused.

— Yeah, Dad, what are you doing?

Dad stared across the room.

— If he's picking on younger boys, maybe he needs a taste of his own medicine.

Nathan looked worried. Ryan stared at Dad.

— Don't, Dad. Sit down, please.

Sophia looked at Dad.

— Yeah, Michael, please sit down. Let's find out what happened.

Dad stared across the room at Deano.

— We heard what happened, Sophia. That massive lump of a boy hit Nathan. I think somebody should have a word with him.

Ryan could feel the tingle of fear mixed with excitement. Nathan looked at him and Ryan could tell he was feeling the same.

Dad pushed Ryan along the seat and on to his feet then started across the room.

— Michael, please!

Sophia gritted her teeth.

— Ryan, Nathan, do something!

Ryan and Nathan watched Dad work his way between tables of people towards Deano. It felt like a film.

Sophia started to breathe heavily.

— Nathan!

Nathan stared across the room, transfixed. Sophia grabbed his arm.

— Nathan Joseph McKenzie, you get up and stop him right now!

Ryan watched Dad tap Deano on the shoulder. Deano turned to face him. Dad was slightly taller, even with Deano's hat, but clearly not as heavy. A woman at the table next to him looked angry. Dad started talking, his hands moving in front of his face. He pointed back towards them and Deano looked over. Ryan and Nathan looked down.

Deano shrugged and turned away from Dad. Dad pulled his shoulder, spinning him back round. Deano shrugged Dad's hand off and pushed him in the chest. Dad stumbled backwards, knocking into an old man eating a hot dog, who looked up and started shouting at Dad. Dad steadied himself, breathed deeply, then charged at Deano, ramming into him, sending them both on to the floor.

Sophia screamed.

— Michael!

Nathan shrugged off her hand and jumped out of his seat and started to run over. Ryan glanced at Sophia, her face pale with shock. He jumped up and followed Nathan.

Dad and Deano were wrestling on the floor, tangled like two sharks. People were standing up at their tables, watching; a few voices were shouting. A baby started to cry.

For a second Ryan felt himself float up above the scene and look down on it. He looked at Nathan. Nathan's eyes were dancing.

Two burly men in chef's clothes waded in and started to pull Dad and Deano apart; somebody booed loudly. Dad's lip was split as he was pulled away. Deano's face was red and dripping with sweat.

Ryan felt his mouth open wide as he stared at Dad. Dad was looking straight at Nathan, breathing heavily. Ryan looked across at Nathan. Nathan was staring back at Dad, his eyes still completely charged.

Ameliah stares through the scratched plastic window of the tape deck. The familiar hiss of static leaks out as she sits cross-legged on her bed, leaning in, waiting for the voice.

— It's different now, you know?

She closes her eyes and smiles as she hears him speak through old plastic and metal.

The room feels hazy from the late-afternoon light through the window. Ameliah presses rewind then stop and play again. Repeating the cycle for the twelfth time.

— It's different now, you know?

She feels her smile getting wider as his voice speaks again. She bangs on her knee with her balled fist.

— I knew it was you.

— Knew it was who?

Ameliah turns to the door. Heather stands with one hand on her hip, a stern look on her face.

— Knew it was who, Am?

Ameliah looks back at the stereo then at Heather.

— Him.

Heather steps into the room.

— Who? Where were you? Why didn't you answer your phone? I waited, you know, like an idiot.

Her face is flushed. Ameliah bites her bottom lip and glances at the mobile phone she dropped on the floor when she got back.

— I'm sorry, I got—

— Distracted, yeah, I figured. It's pretty shitty, Am.

— Something happened.

The hiss of static sounds like breathing then the stereo speaks.

— I miss you.

Heather looks shocked. She stares at the stereo.

— Who's that?

Ameliah looks at her.

— It's my dad.

— It's me. Ryan. No, I'm in Devon. Devon, near the sea. No, I know, sorry, there wasn't enough time, they just sprung it on us. Yeah. Tomorrow, in the afternoon. It took us so long to drive down here. It's all right. Some crazy stuff's happened though. Like, I dunno, my dad fighting an eighteen year old maybe? I'm serious. In a diner, yeah, in front of everyone. I know, it was for Nathan. Just some knobs giving us grief on the beach, it doesn't matter.

— So he did know your dad?

Heather scoops ice cream from the tub in her lap as she sits on the floor next to the bed. Ameliah reaches her arm down from the bed and takes a spoonful.

— Yeah, I think they were pretty good friends. He was at my mum's funeral. He played me this tape that my dad made for him, like a compilation, when they were teenagers and stuff – that's how I knew the voice – it was pretty cool.

Heather looks at her.

— Look at you.

— What?

— You're buzzing.

Ameliah looks at the stereo.

Heather speaks through a mouthful of ice cream.

— No, it's good. I'm just saying, I haven't seen you this excited for a bit.

She looks at the shoeboxes of tapes.

— Your dad loved his tapes, eh?

Ameliah licks her spoon clean.

— Yeah.

— So what's he like, old Joey?

Man, he fully charged this kid, like Gladiators or something, bam, knocking over tables and stuff. You should've seen people's faces. Sophia proper pooed her pants.

Nath? That's the thing, yeah, he loved it. I don't think he thought Dad was capable of doing something like that, you know? I think he thought Dad was just some pushover, I dunno, maybe he was charged by the sea air or something. He was buzzing for hours after. Not Dad, Nathan. Are you listening? Trust me, it was nuts. Look, I'll tell you when I get home. What you been doing? What? In your house? Again? Did you speak to her?

What did you say? Tell me you didn't say anything stupid. Hold on, no, it's the phone, I've gotta put another 20p in. Can you hear me? Yeah, so what did you say? Liam, I know you, there's no way on this earth you said nothing. OK, and that's it? All right, sorry, no, I'm not gonna say that, this is costing me— I am sorry for doubting Big L. He is the supreme master. Shut up, that's enough.

We should get back before four. Yeah, come to mine. Yeah. Wicked. It's been OK, weirdly. Yeah. Seriously, I mean he's still a bit of a knob, but, I dunno, he's all right, kind of. Look, it's beeping again and I've run out of change, I'll call you when we get ho—

Ameliah pictures Joe, hopping across the room to put on the music, the unpacked boxes, the odd socks.

— He's all right. Kinda weird.

Heather takes another scoop.

— Good weird? Or just weird weird?

Ameliah stares at her stretched face in the back of her spoon.

— Good weird. I like him. He's a scientist.

— Like your dad?

— Yeah, kind of, not really, he does nanoscience.

Heather's face goes blank. Ameliah holds up her free hand, squeezing her thumb and index finger together.

— It's all about really, really, really small stuff.

— Like what? Sand?

Ameliah laughs.

— Smaller, microscopic.

Heather scrunches up her face. There's ice cream on her chin.

— And that's his job?

— Yeah, well, his research.

— So he's a nerd?

Ameliah grins.

— Yeah. The highest order of nerd.

She points at Heather and smiles.

— Nice beard.

She watches Heather feel her chin, wipe away the ice cream with her fingers then lick them clean.

— You know he had a stepbrother.

— What?

— My dad, he had a stepbrother that he never mentioned. They didn't speak, some big falling-out before I was born.

— That's crazy.

Heather scrapes the last of the ice cream from the tub.

— Although my mum only found out last Christmas that she had a sister living in Germany.

— You serious?

— Yeah, half-sister or stepsister or whatever. Her dad was in the army and, well, you know. I'm telling ya, Am, our parents.

Downstairs, the phone rings. Ameliah looks at the door. Heather holds her stomach.

— I think maybe I ate too much.

Ameliah looks at her and smiles.

— You think?

She lies down on her back, looking up at the ceiling. Heather does the same on the floor. Downstairs, Nan answers the phone.

Everybody wants you to talk, get stuff out. You should say what you're thinking, Ameliah, tell me what you're feeling, but only when it suits them. When they've carved out a slice of their time to dedicate to you, you're supposed to turn on the tap and just let it all out, then, when time's up, they go on with their lives and you're supposed to just sit in all the crap and sadness you just spewed out.

What If I don't want to talk right now? What if I want to talk at midnight? What if I don't feel like spilling my guts then going for a Big Mac?

I should've listened to you, Dad. This makes so much more sense.

I remember so much. So many moments, but whenever I try to talk, it's like all that comes out are the bad ones.

I'm sitting in the hospital hallway. It smells like school and the lights are hurting my eyes and it's late. Nan brings a hot chocolate back from the machine and we both sit and pretend that it tastes nice and stare at the door and wait and the lady doctor comes out and

her face can't work out what expression to pull and she looks at me and then at Nan and her mouth closes and her lips squash together and for a second it looks like she's got no mouth and Nan leans forward and closes her eyes and I need to hear her say it before I believe it, but I don't want her to speak and I try not to picture you, inside, on your bed, your face all yellow, the bones of your skull, but I can't help it and I can't cry, I can't cry because I can't breathe, cos if I breathe I know I'm gonna throw up.

I know why, Dad, why you went. I know you fought for as long as you did for me. I see that and I'm grateful.

I picture you both now. Like you wanted. Like she wanted.

It's getting better. I mean I don't mean that. I mean it's changing. I can feel it.

I don't want to be treated like a baby. I don't need tucking in at night.

I just want to feel like things can still happen.

CHAPTER 10

— I'm telling you, man, you have to watch it. I'll come with you and see it again. It's that good.

Liam pushed a whole handful of crinkle-cut crisps into his mouth at once, sitting in Ryan's desk chair.

— And you actually see the dinosaurs?

Ryan pulled open his wardrobe door and looked at himself topless in the mirror. Liam crunched crisps with an open mouth.

— See them? They're unbelievable! I've never seen special effects like that. There's this one bit where the guy is on the toilet, yeah, and the T-Rex comes, all angry and that, and, man, I don't wanna spoil it for you, but he eats him, like bang, straight in half, and his legs are hanging and what do you mean, like a mixtape?

— Yeah, but with my voice on there too, in between songs.

Ryan pulled the black T-shirt over his head and stared at himself in the mirror.

297

— This one looks good, right?

Liam reached into his packet again.

— You mean saying stuff?

Ryan looked at him.

— Of course saying stuff. What do you think, that I'm just gonna record myself breathing?

— All right, I was just asking. That'll take ages to make, man.

Liam looked out of the window. Ryan turned his body, checking out his outfit from the side.

— Not really. All I have to do is choose the best songs and write myself a little script so I know what I want to say. It'll be the perfect mixtape and I've got till the end of the holidays till she leaves, right?

He puffed up his chest in the mirror, making no difference to his shape.

— And what will you say?

Liam stared out of the window at the backs of the houses opposite. Ryan moved to the window sill and gazed across at the white back door.

— It's that one, with the white door. It's her nan's house.

Liam strained his eyes.

— Have you got binoculars?

Ryan looked at him.

— You're such a perv.

Liam looked up at Ryan guiltily. Ryan wrinkled his nose then smiled.

— They're not powerful enough, they're stupid Fisher Price kids' ones.

Liam smiled.

— I knew it. You know she was at ours again last night?

Ryan looked at him.

— Did you see her?

Liam shook his head, still looking out of the window.

— Nah, I just heard them, through the wall. They were up proper late.

They both stared at the back of Eve's nan's house.

— I can't believe she saw your pants.

— Yeah, she could've seen a lot more too. I was sitting there all dizzy and stuff, in a towel, man, in the living room, with my Nesquik.

Ryan felt Liam's eyes on him.

— What did you just say?

Liam was sitting up straight in the chair like he'd heard a sudden noise.

— Did you just say Nesquik?

Ryan shrugged.

— Yeah, she made us Nesquik, strawberry, with a spoon.

— Holy crap!

Liam jabbed the air with his finger.

— You did it!

Ryan stared at him, puzzled.

— I did what? What are you talking about?

Liam stood up and laid his big hands on Ryan's shoulders, staring right into his eyes.

— She saw your pants?

Ryan nodded.

— She brought you into her nan's house?

Ryan nodded again, feeling his body shake as Liam pushed him back and forth like a doll.

— And she made you strawberry Nesquik, with a spoon?

Ryan screwed up his face.

— What's your point?

Liam stood up straight and started nodding with his eyes closed.

— Fair play, you did it, man.

Ryan slapped Liam's shoulder. Liam opened his eyes.

— I did what?

— You laid it down.

Liam stuck out his bottom lip as he nodded. Ryan rolled his eyes.

— You're an idiot.

Liam prodded his finger into Ryan's chest and sat back down.

— You're such a dark horse, man. Nearly kill yourself, get your pants out AND get the Nesquik? That's some Zorro-type skills.

Ryan shook his head as he stared out of the window, the fingers of his right hand feeling the smooth shell in his jeans pocket.

There was an unfamiliar knock from the landing. Ryan looked at Liam then they both looked at the door.

Nathan stood awkwardly in the doorway. He saw Liam over Ryan's shoulder and nodded. Liam glanced at Ryan then nodded back. Nathan looked at Ryan.

— What you two doing?

Ryan's eyes narrowed.

— Nothing much.

Nathan smiled with pursed lips.

— Cool.

Ryan just stood there. Liam crunched more crisps. Nathan didn't move.

— You OK, Nath?

Nathan nodded.

— This was on the mat downstairs.

He held out a small piece of lined paper. Ryan could see that it had been folded into itself, making its own little envelope. He read his name. He looked at Nathan. Nathan puffed out his cheeks and raised his eyebrows.

Ryan took the note. Nathan looked over at Liam. Liam stared back.

— So. I'll see you later then.

He knocked both his fists together gently. Ryan nodded. Nathan turned and started down the stairs. Ryan pushed his bedroom door closed and turned to Liam. Liam pulled his most exaggerated confused face. Ryan shrugged.

— I dunno.

He opened out the note to A4 size. Liam sat forward.

— Who's it from?

Ryan read the messy writing.

— Yo! What does it say, man?

— It says meet me at the fence tonight at nine. Important.

He read the words again. Liam rocked back in the desk chair, nodding his head.

— It's from her, isn't it? Check you out, Zorro. Laying it down.

Ryan looked at him as he folded the paper back up and felt his shoulders start to rise.

Ameliah looks out at the green of the park stretching away from her and Heather as they sit on the wooden park bench. In the distance a white dog runs ahead of a lone figure.

— You wanna stop at mine tonight?

Heather looks at her phone as she speaks. Ameliah watches the white dog bound back towards its owner. Heather holds up her phone.

— Look, Simone says they're going ice skating tonight. What d'ya reckon, skating then back to mine for a sleepover?

Ameliah watches the white dog circle behind its owner and set off again. Heather nudges her.

— Come on, Am, you can hold my hand. I'm pretty good.

Ameliah sighs. Heather nudges her again.

— There'll be boys.

Ameliah looks at her.

— Seriously, cute ones, from the college. They hang around there.

Ameliah pictures the boy from the supermarket. She looks at Heather.

— I met a boy.

Heather's eyes widen.

— What!?

Ameliah shuffles in her seat.

— Well, not really met, I mean—

— Woah woah woah woah, back up a second! You met a boy? Where?

Ameliah shrugs.

— In the supermarket. It happened really quickly, we didn't even speak properly.

— What did he look like?

Ameliah pictures his face, smiling at her next to the packets of crisps.

— It doesn't matter.

— You're going red, Am.

Heather grins.

— I can't believe you. How could you not tell me about this? Wait, supermarket? Not the one from the park? The one Simone's after?

Ameliah shrugs.

— I dunno.

Heather's mouth drops open.

— It is! Ha ha, check you out! What did you say to him?

Ameliah looks down.

— I kind of ran off. I mean, yeah. I ran off. I was following Joe, it just happened.

Heather shakes her head.

— Oh, Am, you need some help. Not to worry, if he works at the supermarket, we know something, right? What was his name?

Ameliah looks at her.

— I don't know.

Heather blows air out of her mouth.

— Man, we really do need to start at the beginning. Come tonight, it'll be like practice.

Ameliah looks at her. Heather nods a smile.

— Yeah?

— Yeah. OK, but if Simone starts, I'm leaving.

As she speaks, she feels her phone vibrating next to her stomach. Heather smiles at her as Ameliah pulls it out.

— She's just jealous, you know.

Ameliah reads the word Nan on the small phone screen.

— Yeah? Jealous of what?

Heather lays her hand on Ameliah's shoulder.

— Of your natural beauty.

Heather smiles a cheesy smile. Ameliah shakes her head.

— Shut up, will you? Hi, Nan.

She turns her head away from Heather as she talks into the phone.

— Yeah. I'm in the park, with Heather. We're thinking of going skating later, ice skating and, what? When? Tonight? But I was going to stop at Heather's and, no, yeah, what did he say? Are you OK? I dunno, you sound funny. What does that mean, important? Well, did he say anything else? No, all right. What time? OK, OK, yep. I'll be there. Yes, I promise. See you—

She looks at the phone.

— Well, that was weird.

— What was?

— I can't come tonight. We're going to Joe's.

— Joe's?

— Yeah, for dinner. Apparently he has something important he wants to tell me.

Heather wrinkles her nose.

— Shame, I was looking forward to seeing you trying to skate.

She smiles and pushes Ameliah in the side.

— I wonder what he wants to tell you.

Ameliah stares out at the park. The lone figure and the white dog step out of sight into the tall trees.

The sun cast long chimney-shaped shadows across the pavement into the road. Liam cupped his hands to his mouth, making a basic kick and snare drumbeat as he walked along. Ryan walked beside him, his head nodding as he rhymed.

— I'll put spaghetti in your pocket and call you Mr Pasta. My pocket's full of dough cos it's the bread that I'm after. Laughter, you are just the student, me the master. I cut you to the bone, leave you moaning for a plaster. I'm faster—

He stopped mid-sentence as they turned on to the high street. Liam lowered his hands.

— Don't stop, that was really good.

He looked at Ryan. Ryan stared into space.

— You definitely think that's what she means?

His eyes narrowed. Liam looked at him and smiled.

— Don't be stupid, man. I M P ortant. It's pretty obvious.

Ryan looked up at him. Liam wrapped his arms round his own

body and kissed the air in front of him, making sloppy noises with his mouth.

— Stop it.

Liam stopped.

— Of course that's what she means, Ryan. What's wrong with you?

He lifted his hands up and started to slow dance with no one, singing the word.

— I M Portant.

He bumped Ryan's shoulder with his own. Ryan pictured himself standing in Eve's nan's kitchen, wrapped in a towel, her standing in front of him, her hair blowing behind her, her eyes staring into his. He felt his stomach turn.

— Ryan! You OK? Liam was holding him by the top of his arms.

— You OK, man? You look funny.

Ryan felt his stomach with his hand and thought about digestive acids, the soup of bacteria that live inside everyone. He looked at Liam.

— I need to go home.

Ameliah stares at the old stereo. She pictures Dad, sitting on his bed, her age, recording his voice, his fingertips rubbing his dark hair as he speaks.

She runs her fingers over the front, feeling the cool plastic and metal, the smooth panels and bumpy mesh of the speaker, down to the bedside table and the shell. She picks it up and tries to look through the tiny hole, perfectly drilled. Her eyes focus on the floor beyond the shell, where the shoeboxes full of tapes all sit waiting.

— I'll hear you all. I promise.

— Am! We're going!

Ameliah stands up and slides the shell into her hip pocket.

In the hall, Nan is rummaging around the telephone table, muttering under her breath.

— You OK, Nan?

Nan doesn't look at her.

— I'm fine. Just can't find my bloody keys.

Her voice is harsh and Ameliah knows not to push it.

— Got them. Right, let's go.

Nan strides towards the door. Ameliah follows her. Nan clicks on the hall light and opens the front door.

The short man has his right fist raised like he's giving a 'fight the power' gesture. His brown suede jacket is dated; the white shirt underneath it clings to his barrel body. He looks like a history teacher.

Ameliah sees a small bunch of violet flowers drooping in his left hand.

He looks at Nan.

— Patricia, amazing timing as ever.

Nan raises her hand to her mouth.

— Richard, oh balls.

Richard looks confused. He glances at Ameliah. She smiles politely.

— Am I too early?

His smile is wide. Nan breathes in through her teeth.

— No, no, no, you're right on time, Richard. I'm afraid something's come up. I'm so sorry.

Richard's smile vanishes. He holds up the flowers. Nan looks at them.

— For me? Oh, Richard, you shouldn't have, really. Come on, Ameliah.

She starts past Richard. He steps to the side as Ameliah pulls the front door to. Nan looks back at him.

— I'm sorry, Richard, this is Ameliah, my granddaughter.

Am, say hello to my friend Richard. Look, can we move it to next week, please? I'll cook. I'll cook you a meal you'll never forget, I promise. Come on, Am.

Ameliah waves awkwardly at Richard even though they're close enough to touch. He looks at the flowers in his hand. Ameliah looks at them then at him.

— Am! Let's go!

Nan calls from the other side of the front hedge.

— I'll ring you this weekend, Richard, OK? Honestly, I'm so sorry.

Ameliah watches Nan as they get into the car; her face looks like she's trying to do long division in her head.

— Seat belt on, please.

Nan starts the engine. Ameliah looks out of the window.

— Are we just gonna leave him there?

She stares back at the house. Richard stands frozen on the front step as they drive away.

— You sure you don't want me to stay over? For morale? I could whisper lines to you like in that film.

— What film?

— You know, the one with the guy with the big nose and he wants the girl, but she thinks he's the handsome one, remember?

Ryan looked at Liam, standing in the street, his right fist stuck on his nose, his left hand fanning the air behind him like he was mid fencing match.

— No thanks, I think this one's a solo mission, you know?

Liam lowered his arms and nodded.

— Yeah, course. Call me in the morning though, yeah? Good luck!

Ryan raised his thumb to Liam as they parted ways outside the newsagent. As he walked along the terraced road, he thought about Eve. Her walking up to their front door, looking at the note in her hands before she slid it through the letter box.

He pictured Nathan standing in his bedroom doorway, holding it out. Why didn't Nathan just throw it away? Or leave it? Did he read it?

He remembered the look on Nathan's face as they stood on the beach in front of Deano and his gang. The spark in his eyes as he stood up to a kid nearly twice his size.

As he stepped through the front door, Ryan looked at the round clock on the wall above the bookcase. Seven o'clock. Two hours before he was due to meet Eve. Two hours before something important happened. He smelled dinner as he shut the front door. He told himself he was just hungry as he felt his stomach churn.

— You look pale.

Nathan's voice made him jump. He was sitting in the shadows on the stairs, holding the phone in his lap.

— Don't do that, man.

Ryan breathed out heavily.

— What are you doing?

Nathan looked down at the phone.

— My dad's supposed to call.

Ryan looked back up at the clock.

— How many hours behind is he?

Nathan glanced at the clock as well.

— Eight.

— So it's eleven there then.

Nathan smiled sarcastically.

— Yes, genius.

He shook his head.

— Do you mind?

He nodded towards the living-room door. Ryan looked at the door then back at Nathan.

313

— You know, he did it for me once, my dad I mean. It was at sports day when I was about nine.

Nathan stared at him. Ryan carried on.

— There was this teacher, Mr Towey, he hated me. Anyway, we're all lined up for the hundred metres right, you know, leaning forward, waiting for the whistle, and he's looking at me, and someone falls forward. It wasn't me, but it's a false start and he comes straight over and pulls me by the collar and says I'm disqualified. Just like that.

I'm crying my eyes out and Dad comes over from the side of the track and says it doesn't matter and we should just start again, but Mr Towey is all no, no, he false started, he has to learn the rules. I'm proper blubbing, cos I've been running round the block for weeks, training, timing myself and stuff, and Dad just looks at Mr Towey and says you let my son back in this race or me and you are gonna have a problem.

Nathan's head tilted as he listened. Ryan puffed up his chest, enacting the story.

— Right in his face, in front of all these other parents. My mum was watching too. I look at her in the crowd and she just shrugs, so I turn back and look up at them both and I can see Dad's face and I really believe he's gonna knock this guy out and I can't lie, it felt brilliant.

Nathan stared at him, transfixed.

— And then what?

— What?

— Then what happened?

Ryan sighed.

— That's it really. He let me back in the race, but I was so nervous about false starting I didn't start running till everyone else had gone. I think I was fifth or something. It didn't matter though – seeing that was worth it. You know what I mean?

He felt the warmth of the memory as he looked at Nathan on the stairs. Nathan looked at the phone in his lap.

— Yeah. I do.

Joe's shirt looks like a page from a maths exercise book. He has clearly made an effort with his hair, the edges of the bird's nest tamed with some kind of hair product.

He hovers in the doorway, smiling awkwardly. Ameliah and Nan stand on the step in front of him.

— Come in, sorry, thanks for coming.

Ameliah sees him glance at Nan and nod. The air feels thick as he follows them up the dark stairs.

The flat has been tidied, kind of. The boxes and bags pushed against the far wall, the tapes and CDs stacked neatly and the old table has been pulled out and is covered with what looks like an old curtain. A plastic bottle of table salt sits alone in the middle.

Ameliah scans the room for the old stereos and finds them in the corner under the window. Light from the tall standard lamp warms the floor and she pictures the spare room.

— I hope you ladies like Italian.

His voice is trying too hard.

— Sit down. I mean, please.

He shepherds them into the room. Ameliah and Nan sit on the edge of the sofa. Nan looks around.

— Nice place.

She glances at Ameliah. Ameliah shrugs. Joe looks round the room.

— Yeah, I mean it's early days, but I think it'll scrub up well. It's got amazing acoustics.

He swirls his finger like he's balancing a plate.

— An amazing what?

Nan looks confused. Ameliah lays her hand on Nan's knee.

— The sound, Nan. He means sounds sound nice in here.

Joe points at Ameliah.

— Exactly. I think it's the shape. I mean most of these old buildings have thick walls so they absorb more and it just gives this kind of, I dunno, warmth, you know?

He looks at them both, clearly nervous. Ameliah offers a smile. Nan nods.

— Yes, I'd love a drink, thank you, Joe.

Joe clicks his fingers.

— Of course, what will you have? I've got beer, wine, vodka?

Nan smiles politely.

— A wine will be fine, thanks.

Joe nods and starts out of the room. He stops himself and looks back at Ameliah.

— And you? No vodka of course.

He chuckles. Nan looks at him.

— She'll have a soft drink, Joe.

Joe smiles nervously.

— Yeah, right, one wine, one soft drink, coming up.

He slips out of the room to the kitchen. Ameliah

breathes out. She stares at the dark screen of the TV, seeing her and Nan's reflection warped like in the back of a spoon.

— What's going on, Nan. Is he OK? What do you think he meant by important?

Nan's face looks like she's thinking two things at once.

— I don't know, love. Let's just see, shall we? Give him a chance?

She scans the room.

— Something tells me he's not exactly used to entertaining.

Ameliah smiles and nods.

— People skills. He's trying though.

Nan smiles back.

— Yes, love, we'll give him that.

Joe comes back into the room holding a pint glass half full of red wine and a dark mug with white letters on the side.

— There you go. You'll have to excuse the cups. I haven't really had a chance to stock up my cupboards, but a drink's a drink, right?

Ameliah smiles as she takes the mug and reads the chemical symbol for water. Nan forces a smile as she takes the pint glass. Joe stands there. Ameliah and Nan sip their drinks.

— Music! Stupid. One second.

He reverses away from them and stumbles over the edge of a white sports bag, regaining his balance and carrying on to the stereo under the window. Ameliah watches Nan screw her face up at the wine.

She feels the need to help Joe out, but doesn't know how. She pictures him getting ready in the mirror earlier, wrestling his scruffy hair with a comb, then the sound of a saxophone grabs her ears.

She stares at the tall speaker next to the TV as Joe walks back over holding a wooden chair that looks like he stole it from a school.

The saxophone breathes out of the speaker like smoke and Ameliah pictures the old stereo back in her room. She thinks about Mum and imagines her lying on her bed, her eyes closed, listening to the music.

— John Coltrane.

Joe and Nan both look at her, surprised. Nan's eyes narrow.

— You know Coltrane?

Ameliah shakes her head and shrugs.

319

— Not really. I found a tape.

She watches Nan drift into a memory. Joe coughs roughly and Nan snaps out of it.

Ameliah sees Joe look at Nan and widen his eyes. Nan looks back at him, her face serious. Joe makes a big deal of rolling his eyes and slapping his thigh.

— Dessert! I forgot. I'm such an idiot. I meant to pick something up.

Nan cuts in.

— Am will go, won't you, love?

Ameliah looks out through the bay window. The last of the sunlight clings to the sky. She looks at Nan. Nan shrugs.

— The supermarket should still be open, on the high street. It's not dark yet. It's not far.

Ameliah hears the word supermarket and pictures the boy with the dark eyes. Nan fishes inside her purse and pulls out a ten-pound note. Ameliah looks across at Joe. He smiles nervously.

— Course. What shall I get?

She puts her mug on the floor next to the sofa and stands up, taking the note and stuffing it into her jeans pocket. Nan shakes her head.

— It doesn't matter, you choose.

Ameliah feels light as she walks between them, the saxophone notes floating round her, fading away as she walks out of the room and down the stairs.

Ryan stared at himself in the small circular bathroom mirror and tried to imagine his face with a beard. He felt his smooth chin with the inside of his fingers and wondered what it would feel like when he started to shave.

He reached for the toothpaste and his brush and squeezed a small ball on to the bristles.

As he brushed in the mirror, he remembered sitting on the edge of the bath with Mum, both of them chewing the chalky red tablets that show up how dirty your teeth really are. He looked down into the sink and remembered the red foam that they spat out against the white porcelain. How Mum had said they were vampires back home from a fresh hunt for blood.

He stared at his frothing white mouth in the mirror as he brushed and thought about the baddies from James Bond films who bite concealed cyanide capsules rather than be captured.

The door banged loudly. Ryan spat as Nathan's voice came through it.

— Hurry up, man! I need to pee.

Ryan rinsed his mouth and opened the door. Nathan groaned.

— About time. I was about to just go and pee on your bed.

Ryan smiled sarcastically.

— Yeah, right.

Nathan looked at him.

— Are you going to bed already?

— No.

— So why are you brushing your teeth?

Ryan shifted his feet.

— Cos I felt like it. What do you care?

Nathan shrugged.

— I don't. Move.

He pushed past him and shoved him out of the bathroom, slamming the door and locking it. Ryan held his hand up to his face and breathed out with his mouth then in through his nose.

He stuck out his bottom lip and nodded to himself as he walked back into his room.

— I can see you. I'm waving. Across the road.

Heather's voice is excited. Ameliah keeps the mobile next to her ear and stares across the road. Heather is waving her arms wildly, standing at the bus stop with Simone.

— Come over.

— I've got to go to the supermarket. They sent me for a cake or something.

— You cross the road right now. I'm hanging up.

Ameliah watches Heather dramatically mime hanging up her mobile as she crosses the road. She feels Simone staring at her as she slips her phone back into her front pouch and pulls her hood over her head.

— How funny, right?

Heather beams. Ameliah nods.

— He does live just round the corner.

Simone cuts in.

— Who does?

Heather looks at Simone.

— Joe. He's Am's friend, well, Am's dad's friend. She's there with her nan.

Simone looks Ameliah up and down.

— Hanging out with old men and your nan on a

Friday night now, Ameliah?

Ameliah looks at Heather.

— I'll see you later.

As she goes to walk away, she sees two older boys coming towards them. Both of them wear New Era caps and dark jackets. Ameliah recognises the boy from the supermarket straight away; his smooth skin and thin body make him look younger than his chunkier friend. Simone and Heather spot the pair and Simone brushes her hair behind her ear, pouting her lips as she moves towards them. The two boys stand at the end of the bus stop. The bigger one lights a cigarette.

— Let's have one of your fags.

Simone's voice is cocky as she points. The boys both look at her. The bigger one shrugs and holds out the cigarette. Simone takes it and stands next to him, staring at his friend.

— I'm Simone.

Ameliah watches the boy from the supermarket shrug. The bigger boy looks at Simone.

— Hello, Simone, I'm Kyle.

Simone ignores him and stares at his friend.

— And what's your name?

The boy from the supermarket looks at Simone.

— You know you shouldn't smoke, Simone, it's bad for you.

He looks at Heather and then at Ameliah. His eyes light up.

— It's you.

Heather and Simone stare at Ameliah. Simone is frowning hard. Ameliah digs her hands into her front pouch, hiding in her hoody. The boy from the supermarket walks straight past Simone and Heather and stands in front of her, an arm's length away. Ameliah can see his eyes clearly now. His lean face under his dark cap.

He smiles.

— You gonna run off again?

Ameliah looks at him. She can feel Heather and Simone staring. He holds out his hand.

— I'm Malik.

She looks at his slender fingers and imagines them playing the piano or wrapping a present. She holds out her hand and lets him take it. His skin is cold and smooth. She smiles.

— I'm Ameliah.

Malik's smile widens.

— I knew it would be something good.

Ameliah feels her knees pressing the inside of her jeans as he reaches up and delicately pulls back her hood. She looks down and bites her bottom lip.

— You shouldn't hide in that thing. Trust me.

His voice is calm and deep. Ameliah glances at Heather. Heather sticks her tongue into the inside of her cheek and smiles. Ameliah looks back at Malik, her hand in his the whole time.

CHAPTER 11

The shell felt cold and smooth as Ryan turned it over in his hand. The light was fading and, as he looked up at the sky, he thought about people on the other side of the world getting ready to start their day.

He leaned forward and looked through the slit where the fences met. The other garden was empty, the long grass like dirty polar bear fur.

— Where are you?

He felt his stomach churning as he whispered. A shaft of light cut down the grass as the white back door opened. Ryan saw a shadow step into the light then everything went dark again. He stood up straight, his blood charged like he was on the starting line of a race. He pushed the shell back into his pocket and waited.

— You OK?

Eve didn't answer. He could hear her breathing on the other side. He thought about how it could happen. Would he have to climb up again? Maybe she could get the wheelbarrow and they could both sit up on the fence. What if they fell? He decided that a kiss would be worth it as he noticed how dry his throat felt.

— Eve? You all right?

— Not really.

Ryan felt himself deflate as she spoke. He stared at the gap and tried to make her out.

— What is it?

The fence swayed slightly as she leaned on it from the other side.

— My mum's here.

Ryan thought he heard a sniff. He leaned on his side of the fence and pretended it wasn't there.

— That's good, right?

— No.

— Why not?

He moved his ear right next to the gap.

— She moved out. They're finished.

Ryan looked down as he heard her broken breathing.

— Are you sure?

He shook his head at how stupid a question that was.

— Sorry, I mean that's rubbish.

— Yeah. I knew it was coming, but yeah, it is.

She blew out a sigh and he pictured her wiping tears from her face.

— We're leaving.

Ryan felt his legs go heavy.

— When?

— In the morning.

Ryan thought he might fall over.

— No. I mean you can't.

— Yeah, we can. Mum's taking me back – there's things to sort out. She's in there now watching a film with my nan like everything's OK.

Ryan felt a lump in his throat. He looked down and saw the white shell in his hand.

— Stupid.

— John Wayne. I hate John Wayne. What did you say?

Ryan shook his head.

— I said stupid. Parents are stupid.

He threw the shell on to the ground behind him.

— I wanted to speak to you, before we left.

— What about your tape?

— What tape?

Her face was pressed against the gap and Ryan could see her eye looking straight at him.

— I was going to make you a mixtape. My favourite songs. It was going to be perfect, but now there's no time.

He felt his hands balling into fists. He could see the corner of her mouth through the gap.

— I'm sorry, Ryan. I'm sure it would've been the best mixtape ever.

Ryan shrugged.

— Yeah, well. I guess the universe is full of it after all.

— Don't say that.

— It's true. Why throw us together then take you away?

He heard Eve sigh.

— I don't know. Maybe it's the wrong time.

He could hear the defeat in her voice.

He puffed out his cheeks, fighting the tears he could feel forming.

— Did you bring me a shell?

— What?

— A shell, from the sea.

— Shit!

He spun round and scanned the lawn for the discarded shell.

— Are you OK?

He started to scramble around on all fours, sweeping the ground with his hand like a metal detector.

— Yes! Hold on! I've got one. It's a good one. Come on, where is it?!

— It doesn't matter.

— NO! I've got it! Just wait a second! Yes!

He felt relief wash over him as his fingertips touched the smooth shell.

— Here. All the way from the sea.

He turned the shell on its side and slotted it through the gap. He felt her fingertips on his as she took it from him. He left his hand there, not wanting to let go.

— Do you like it?

He felt her hold the end of his fingers on the other side.

— It's perfect.

Ryan imagined ripping the fence out of the ground and throwing it away, over the roof of the house, and wrapping his arms around her.

— I'm gonna make a necklace with it.

Her hand felt warm.

— A necklace?

— Yeah, you drill a hole and thread the string through. You have to be careful that it doesn't shatter.

— And you can do that?

— Yeah.

Ryan looked up at the dark sky. He couldn't see the moon. He thought about Liam, kissing the air in the street.

— Important.

He shook his head and felt Eve squeeze his finger.

— What's important?

— No, I mean your note said important and Liam thought, it doesn't matter, he's an idiot.

— What did he think?

— Nothing.

— Tell me.

Ryan scrunched up his face.

— He thought it meant you wanted me to kiss you.

He felt his hand moving up the gap as she pulled it.

— *Psssssst.*

He looked up to the top of the fence and saw Eve's face, her chin resting on the dark wood.

— How are you doing that?!

Eve smiled and looked down.

— I reckon if you get your foot in that gap and push up you can reach me.

Ryan jammed his foot into the crack in the fence and heaved.

He felt the air on his face as he pushed himself up so his eyes were level with hers. He looked at her. She smiled and leaned towards him and—

— Eve! Eve!

Ryan felt his body wobble as Eve pulled her hand away. He gripped the top of the fence. He watched the light cut down the lawn as the back door opened. He ducked his head down, still suspended by his foot in the gap.

— What are you doing out here?

The woman's voice was stern.

— Nothing, Mum. I just, I left something here earlier. I'm coming.

Ryan watched through the gap as Eve started up the garden towards the house. The woman in the doorway stepped out on to the patio.

— Come on, sweetheart, we still need to finish packing. You OK? Did you find what you were looking for?

Ryan watched Eve look back down the garden towards him, the light from inside the kitchen framing her. He saw her hand hold up the shell.

— Yeah. I found it.

Ameliah can hear Nan's muffled voice through the kitchen door, talking to Joe, and she remembers hearing Mum and Dad through her bedroom floor. The pair of them giggling like kids as they watched their film. She stares at the stack of CDs, scanning the spines for the name of a band she recognises. She pictures Simone's face earlier at the bus stop. Her and Heather watching in amazement as Malik typed her mobile number into his phone.

— You find anything?

She looks up at Joe, his face flushed from the wine. His eyes are glazed as he smiles at her.

— Not yet, maybe you should choose?

He shakes his head.

— Come on, DJ, it's your job. There's more in that bag.

He points to a dark holdall near the bookcase with his finger, still holding his glass, then heads to the sofa. Ameliah can hear Nan banging plates in the kitchen.

— So my dad got you into hip hop?

She looks over her shoulder at Joe. He sips from his glass and looks back.

— Yeah. Eventually. We didn't always get along, you know?

He takes another sip.

— It was hard.

Ameliah starts looking through the CDs in the dark bag. She hears Nan humming louder in the kitchen as she pulls out a brown notebook.

— You know what teenagers are like, right? I mean you are one.

Joe speaks to her back as she opens the notebook. A photograph slides out on to her knees, the gloss image catching the light.

— By the time we went to college we were friends.

Ameliah doesn't hear him. Her eyes are fixed on the faces in the photograph. Mum is younger, wearing tight jeans and a dark vest top as she smiles and reaches out her arms, across what looks like a dance floor, to Joe. He's younger too, the edges of his scruffy hair stuck to the side of his face with sweat, his eyes fixed on her.

Ameliah feels her skin go cold.

— Found anything? Come on, this party's starting to fade.

335

She feels his eyes on her back as she turns over the photograph and reads the words:

Nath,
Me and you, going for it! Leeds 99
love Eve x

She can feel her ribs under her skin as she turns round.

She holds up the photo, telling herself not to blink. Joe squints at her.

— What is it?

— Nath, me and you, going for it! Leeds 99, love Eve.

His face drops as she speaks. Ameliah stands up, her eyes not leaving him as she walks towards the sofa.

— That's an old photo.

He sits forward, perching on the edge of the sofa.

— From university, he continues, you weren't supposed to—

— You're Nathan?

Ameliah stares at him.

— Let me explain.

— You're Nathan?!

— Please let me—

336

— What are you doing with my mum?

— Ameliah.

— Were you having an affair?

— What? No, don't be ridiculous. Come and sit down, let me explain, please.

He stands up and Ameliah steps back.

— Where was my dad? Did he know? Your own stepbrother?

Joe steps towards her.

— Ameliah, please, it's complicated. Your dad wasn't even around then.

Ameliah holds up her hand. Joe stands still.

— That was university. I met her at university, read the date.

Ameliah looks at the photograph. Mum's face smiling as she dances.

— She wasn't with your dad. Not then. Not yet. Not properly.

Ameliah kneels down on the floor. She thinks about Mum, telling her the story. How she was at university when Dad just showed up. How she knew it was him. How she still had the necklace. She reaches into her hip pocket and pulls out the shell.

Joe sits down, his legs crossed in front of him on the floor, just out of arm's reach.

— I've been trying to tell you. It's hard, you know. What's that?

Ameliah looks at him and holds up the shell. Joe bites his lip.

— You have it. Course you have it.

Ameliah squeezes the shell in her hand.

— I don't understand. Who's Joe?

Joe sighs.

— Joe is me.

— What?

— I mean, yeah, I'm Nathan, but I'm Joe too. Nathan Joseph McKenzie. Joe is my middle name.

Ameliah feels her head swimming.

— Why did you lie?

— It's complicated. Look, Ameliah, I'm sorry. I thought it was for the best if you didn't know who I was. I didn't know what your dad had told you, we said some things before I left, I just, I thought maybe if I was a stranger it would be, I dunno, I'm—

He looks down into his drink. Ameliah stares at the photograph.

— We met at uni, in Leeds. There was this place, this little club where they had these open mic nights. I saw her onstage.

— With her guitar?

— Yeah. This one night I'm watching and she just comes on and . . .

He glances at the ceiling.

— She was amazing, Ameliah.

Ameliah looks down at the photo, at younger Joe's eyes on Mum.

— We got together somehow, I mean it took a while. I wouldn't leave her alone. It was after Christmas, spring term, she gave in and we hooked up. We used to go dancing, in that same club, the one in the photo. It was like a cave. We danced, man, we'd dance all night.

Ameliah watches him play memories over in his head.

— And then my dad showed up.

Joe comes back from his memory and looks at her. His face straightens.

— Exactly. Out of the blue. Just for a visit. I sometimes wonder what would've happened if he hadn't driven up, you know? If we hadn't figured our crap out and started actually getting on, he wouldn't have visited me at all. I dunno, maybe if he'd even come up the next weekend or something. I know you can't think like that, things happen, but your mind, your mind won't leave it alone.

He shakes his head.

— How the hell was I supposed to know? We never spoke about her. I mean I knew there was a girl and that she left. I knew that much, but I never knew her name, why would I? We were so young. She moved around so much he couldn't keep in touch with her, I dunno. It was different then, nobody had a computer.

His eyes narrow.

— Of all the girls, I mean all the girls anywhere, and I pick the one who still wears the necklace a boy gave her when she was fourteen.

Ameliah looks at him.

— He didn't give her a necklace.

— What?

— He gave her the shell. She made the necklace. I know the story.

Joe sniffs and straightens his back. He blows out air and taps his fists together gently.

— OK, well, whoever made it, she was still wearing it. Them's the breaks, right? I can remember the look on her face, you know, when he walked in? His face too. And that was that.

Ameliah stares at him.

— You're the other guy.

He forces a smile. She can see tears in his eyes.

— That's me. Who was I to get in the way of a fairy tale?

He swigs the last of his wine.

— I need another drink.

Ameliah watches him as he stands up.

— So that's what you argued about?

Joe tilts his head.

— I guess that's one way of putting it, yeah. You know I remember thinking at the time, so what? You know? So he gave you a shell, years ago, what's the big deal?

Ameliah takes a deep breath.

— The universe.

Joe looks at her.

— What did you say?

She stares up at him. She pictures Mum sitting on

the edge of her bed, telling her that people find people all the time. That the tiniest parts of everything that's alive are made up of particles that are either attracted to or repel each other.

— The universe calls the shots.

Joe's mouth tries to smile as he sits back down on the floor.

— Yeah, the universe. And the tape.

His head drops forward as he sighs. Ameliah sits back on her heels.

— What tape?

Joe looks up.

— Your dad's tape. The tape he made for her that night, when he was thirteen.

Ameliah shakes her head.

— What tape?

— The deal clincher. The tape of him speaking, talking about the universe and how they were meant to be and all that stuff, I don't know. You know what's messed up? You know what really twisted the knife when I was miles away thinking about it? I helped.

— What do you mean?

— I mean I helped him. That night. I didn't have any

clue what I was helping him with really, but I helped. I know I did.

Ameliah pictures the old tape. The battered dark plastic. The torn label with the broken blue letters. Joe wipes his mouth with the back of his hand.

— He didn't know what to do. The only tape he had was the one for his mum and there was no time. He hit me, you know? Your dad. Little Ryan actually hit me in the face. I was such an idiot.

Ameliah looks at him and feels herself wanting to move closer. Joe smiles.

— Like a movie, right? The chance had passed, she's leaving, that was it, story over, until the hero seizes the day and does his thing. Sneaks out, stone on window, gives her the tape, they kiss, roll end credits. I don't know what he said on that tape, but whatever it was, it worked.

Ameliah pictures sitting behind Mum and Dad in the car. The three of them driving along a narrow road in Ireland. Dad looking at Mum, Mum smiling back. Like they both knew something that nobody else did.

She moves forward on her knees, stopping at arm's length from Joe.

He taps his fists together slowly. Ameliah tries to picture him younger, watching the girl he wanted see her first love, his stepbrother, walk into the room after years of thinking she'd lost touch forever. Her fingers reaching for the necklace she made with the shell he gave her. Like a film. She pictures Joe struggling to know where to look.

— Then what happened?

— Then I left. That's what happened. They had each other and I didn't really fancy sticking around to watch the rest of that movie, to be honest.

— To America?

— Yeah. My course let you study away, so I applied and I went. She got pregnant with you pretty much straight away I guess.

He shrugs.

— Other side of the world. Everything was fine. I had a life. There were people, women, I mean Jesus, I was even engaged once. It took me a while but I moved on. That's what you do, right?

He shakes his head.

— We fought. Me and your dad. It was stupid. I said some stuff, he said some stuff back, your mum tried to

help, but she just made it worse really. Miles away just
felt like the best thing for everyone.

He rubs his hands down his face.

— Then she has to go and die.

Joe shakes his head again.

— Look, Ameliah, I never meant—

— So you were arguing about Mum? At the funeral?

She pictures Joe standing in the back garden of the
old house at Mum's funeral. Looking at Dad. His face
angry and confused.

— Yeah, well, no, not really.

— What do you mean?

— He just dropped it on me. Years of not speaking,
miles apart and all the crap we'd been carrying for all
that time, and there we are, at her funeral, which I
wasn't even sure I should go to, and he tells me about
the cancer. Can you imagine that? At a funeral. He tells
me he's dying and asks for my help. For him and your
mum. That he's not sure how long he has, but that the
doctors have told him eighteen months. What do you
say to that? What do you say to a dying man who asks
you to look out for his little girl?

He looks at her.

— I'm here, Ameliah. I'm here cos Ryan asked me to be and I don't even know what I'm doing.

He rubs his eye with the palm of his hand. Ameliah feels herself wanting to help him. This man with odd socks. This man who grew up with her dad. She leans forward.

— Do you have any Tribe Called Quest?

Joe looks at her. She smiles. He smiles back and points to a pile of CDs stacked under the old table.

Ryan threw clothes over his shoulder as he frantically dug through his drawers. His eyes scanned his room, looking for anywhere he might have put a blank tape.

— Come on, come on!

He dived down to the floor and shuffled his body under the bed, his hands reaching out, flipping over old shoes and comics.

He dragged himself back out and smacked his head on the wooden bed frame.

— *Shit!*

He stood up, rubbing his head. His eyes fell on his boom box. The clear plastic window of tape deck two. He sat on the edge of his bed and pressed eject, sliding the dark cassette out and holding it in his hand. He stared at the word he'd written nearly two years ago, when he started recording his voice. He thought about Dad sitting on his bed, telling him he thought it was a brilliant idea. That it could be his way of speaking to her, not for anyone else.

Ryan shook the tape in his hand. He wanted so badly to record something for Eve, something for her to take with her, to remember him by, but this was Mum's tape, his tape for Mum. He closed his eyes, feeling his brain pushing against the inside of his skull as he gritted his teeth.

— Help!

He threw the cassette across the room, hearing it hit the radiator as he opened his eyes and saw Nathan standing in the doorway.

— What do you want?!

— You're shouting.

— No I'm not.

— Yeah you are, you just shouted help! They probably heard it downstairs.

Ryan looked at the floor. Dad and Sophia would be on the sofa, deep into their Friday night film.

— Yeah, well, so what?

347

He rubbed his eyes with his knuckles. Nathan stepped into the room.

— What's going on?

— You know what, Nath, don't, yeah? Just don't. I'm looking for something and I haven't got time for your stupid little digs, all right?

Nathan raised his eyebrows.

— What's this? Angry Ryan? Where did he come from?

Ryan moved to his desk and started rummaging under papers and books.

— Seriously, Nathan, I'm not in the mood, so if you're here to annoy me, just piss off, yeah?

Nathan sat down on the end of the bed.

— Wow. What happened? Did your girlfriend have some bad news? What's her name anyway, Ryanetta?

Ryan looked at him. Nathan smiled his sarcastic smile. Ryan felt his blood get hot, his legs started to shake and before he knew what was happening he was on top of Nathan on the bed, swinging wildly with his hands. Nathan yelped as he caught him in the face with an open hand. He felt the heat in his fingers as he pulled at Nathan's collar, his legs wrapping around his body.

— What are you doing, Ryan?!

Nathan forced his arms down to his side and held him in a

bear hug. Ryan wriggled, trying to force his way out with his neck muscles.

Nathan squeezed him tighter and the bones in Ryan's arms dug into his own ribs. He felt an urge and went with it.

— *Get off!*

Nathan screamed as Ryan sank his teeth into his shoulder.

Ryan's jaw clamped down harder on Nathan's skin. The pair of them rolled over, their momentum taking them off the edge of the bed, and hit the floor with a thud. Ryan groaned, feeling all the air leave his chest as Nathan landed on top of him.

Nathan pinned him down, trapping his arms under his knees, and pulled his arm back to punch. Ryan stared up at him as he fought for breath. He prepared himself for the pain, biting his teeth together. Nathan stared back, his cheeks flushed, tears in his eyes.

— Ryan.

He lowered his arm, falling sideways off Ryan, and slumped on to the floor.

Ryan sat up slowly, feeling the muscles in his stomach. He shook his head and licked his lip, tasting blood.

Nathan stared at the floor, breathing heavily.

— Boys! You OK up there?

Sophia's voice called out from the hall downstairs.

Ryan looked at Nathan. Nathan lifted his head and stared at him.

— We're fine, Mum! Just messing about.

— Ryan! You OK?

Ryan stared at Nathan as he called back.

— Yeah! He's right, we're just messing about! Sorry!

— Well, just be careful, OK!

The living-room door closed. Ryan licked the blood from his lip. Nathan rubbed his shoulder with his hand.

— I could've knocked you out you know.

Ryan looked at him.

Nathan pulled at his T-shirt, trying to look at his neck.

— I can't believe you bit me. Who bites?

Ryan shrugged and stuck out his bloody bottom lip.

— What can I say? That's pretty much my first ever fight.

Nathan looked at him.

— What did you lose?

— I can't find the blank tape. I thought I had one.

— What for?

Ryan sighed.

— She's leaving. I had a plan but I don't have time. I just wanted to do something. I doesn't matter now.

— When does she go?

— In the morning. Her mum's come to get her.

— What about that one?

Nathan pointed to the floor near the radiator. Ryan stared at Mum's tape lying on the carpet. The dark plastic against the chocolate brown. He felt his shoulders drop.

— That one's taken.

Nathan shrugged.

— So tape over it.

Ryan shook his head and looked down.

— I can't.

Nathan wiped his mouth with the back of his hand.

— Fine, but she'll be gone, and you'll wish you had.

— Leave it, Nath, yeah?

Nathan stared at him. Ryan thought about Mum and stared back. Nathan started to get up.

— OK. I'm just saying. When people leave and you don't tell them what you want to before they go, it feels rubbish.

Ryan looked up at him. Nathan nodded.

— Trust me.

Nathan walked out of the room. Ryan stared at the empty door frame. He could feel the pain in his ribs. He thought about Eve, her face in the moonlight at the fence. He thought about the universe, what she'd said. He thought about luck, the random chance that put people together. Mum believed in luck. He turned and stared at Mum's tape. The rectangle of matt-black plastic that had so much of him in it and, as he felt the air filling his lungs, he knew what he had to do.

The engine cuts off.

Ameliah feels Nan's eyes on her as she stares out of the passenger window at the dark houses on their road. She touches the shell in her hoody pocket as she hears the keys in Nan's hand and stares at the front door of the house she now calls home.

— You could have told me.

She turns to Nan. Nan nods.

— I know, love, I'm sorry, but it wasn't really my call. She sighs.

— I know it's a lot to take in, but you have to remember he's trying to do the right thing, like your dad asked him to. It's a big responsibility looking out for someone else's kid, especially when you're—

— The other guy.

Ameliah looks at Nan's face. The tiny crow's feet at

the corners of her eyes. The lines that run from her nostrils to her mouth. Nan nods.

— I think he's a good man. Even if he can't cook for toffee.

Ameliah pictures Joe, looking back at her, knowing he was keeping his promise.

— I like him.

Nan smiles.

— Me too. If you ask me though, it's us who need to be looking out for him. Did you see that place?

Ameliah smiles back.

— Yeah. We should buy him a pair of socks that match.

Nan looks out through the windscreen.

— I think it might be good for us, you know? New chapter. Us girls need a challenge.

She lays her hand on Ameliah's thigh. Ameliah puffs out her cheeks.

— Are things always so complicated?

Nan smiles, still staring out.

— One thing on top of another. So many layers.

Nan leans in.

— Don't worry, love, the right thing to do sticks out when you need it to.

Ameliah looks into Nan's eyes, the dark of her pupils, and pictures the old stereo. The smooth black plastic, those thick buttons. She bites her bottom lip.

— Did you know about the tape?

— What tape?

— Dad made Mum a tape, before she left, I mean before you left.

Nan shakes her head.

— I didn't know about any tape. All I remember is her crying that night before we left, and that shell. You know she made me take her to a jeweller to have the hole drilled. The way the man in the shop looked at me. She never took that thing off, wherever we moved to, and we moved a lot. But when she got something in her head, well, you know what she was like. She never mentioned a tape. Doesn't surprise me though, with your mum and dad nothing surprises me.

Ameliah watches Nan's face start to drift into another memory. She turns and looks up at the house and, as she breathes in, she pictures the old stereo.

Ryan sat on the edge of his bed, staring at his boom box. The black plastic and silver edges. He felt the inside of his split lip with his tongue. The house was quiet. He pictured Nathan, in his bed, staring up at Bruce Lee on his wall. He thought about how funny it was that the people who aren't even trying to help somehow help the most.

He thought about Eve, in her bed, in the back bedroom, half a football pitch away, staring up at her ceiling, wondering what was going to happen when she got back to Ireland. He thought about pushing down against the fence with his foot, his body rising up, bringing his face level with hers, her smile. He thought about her getting ready to leave in the morning, looking out from her bedroom window, across the gardens at his.

He thought about Mum. Her face as she sat on his bed and told him that she was sick. Him having questions but not speaking, just staring at her mouth as she spoke.

He reached out his hand to tape deck two, glancing at his alarm clock. The red digital numbers read 00:19, the same colour as the recording light as he felt the thick buttons click in.

Ameliah sits on the edge of her bed, staring at the old cassette in her hands. The dark scratched plastic, the torn label. She pictures Dad, standing in his dark suit, biting his bottom lip as he stares out at the people at Mum's funeral. She imagines him at the back door, talking to his stepbrother, the stepbrother he hadn't seen for over ten years, whose heart he broke when he stole the girl. The pair of them arguing, Nathan telling Dad it was too much of an ask, that he wasn't up to it, Dad asking again, telling him he was ill, asking him to look out for her, his little girl, Eve's little girl, to be there for her if she needed him. How could he not?

She thinks about younger Dad, sitting on the edge of his bed, like she is right now, leaning in, recording his thoughts. The thoughts that let Mum know he was for her, that made her keep the shell, make the necklace, layer upon layer of the story that led to her, Ameliah, being here.

She looks at her watch. The digital numbers read 12:19. She pushes eject and slides the tape into the deck, then closes it. Her fingers move down and press the thick play and record button at the same time. She takes a deep breath as the red light comes on.

— Hello? Is it on? Yeah, I can see the light. It's on. I'm recording. Hello. Who am I saying hello to? You. I'm saying hello to you. This was your idea, remember?

— Remember what?

Ameliah stares at the speaker. She closes her eyes and shakes her head.

— This is what you did. I'm sorry it took me this long. I didn't get it before, but I do now—

— Who's there?

She stops breathing, her eyes fixed on the little red light.

— Hello?

— Who is that? Can you hear me?

Ameliah closes her eyes.

— Are you talking to me? Hello? This is Ryan Wilson. I think I'm somehow tuned into your frequency, I think it happened before. Can you hear me?

She takes a deep breath, trying to stay calm.

— Yes.

— OK, good. Who are you?

— Dad?

— What? You're breaking up, can you hear me?

— Yeah, I can hear you.

— OK. I'm not sure how this is happening, maybe it's the aerials or something. Where are you?

— Are you recording?

— Yeah, how did you know?

— I'm recording too.

Ameliah feels her heart thumping in her chest.

— We're both recording.

— Where are you?

— I'm in my room. Just like you.

— What?

— You're recording for her.

— Hold on, what? You're breaking up.

The speakers hiss with static.

— How do you know that? Who are you?

Ameliah stares at the cogs of the cassette turning. She can feel the pulse of her blood in her neck.

— You're doing the right thing. She's gonna love it. Eve is gonna love it. She won't forget.

— What? Who are you? How do you know that?

— Trust me. It might take a while but you'll be together. The universe wants you to be together.

— Universe? Who are you?

— I'm Ameliah.

The static creeps out from the speakers again.

— Are you serious?

— Yeah.

— That was my mum's name.

Ameliah leans in and smiles.

— I know.

Ryan looked up at the dark bedroom window, gripping the tape in his left hand. The garden was quiet and, apart from a couple of windows a few houses down with lights still on, the backs of the terraced houses were lit only by the moon.

He felt his stomach flip like when the car went over a hump-back bridge as he reached down to the edge of the patio and picked up a small piece of chipped mortar.

His eyes were starting to sting with tiredness as he drew back his arm, aimed and let fly.

He felt a burst of pride that he'd hit it first shot then realised that the sound of stone hitting glass was quite loud and quickly moved to the fence, staring up.

The dark window stayed lifeless, like the mouth of a cave that he knew something lived in. He told himself that a minute was a good length of time to wait before trying again and started to count under his breath, the whole time staring up.

The fence behind him creaked and he jumped forward. The fat gargoyle cat stared down at him and he let out a sigh of relief.

— No wonder you've got no mates.

He stared at the cat as he whispered then looked up at the window, thinking he saw something move. The dark window stayed lifeless.

He turned back to the cat.

— Now I've lost count. Nice one.

Moonlight bounced back from the cat's eyes as it blinked slowly then the kitchen light clicked on. Ryan ducked down, moving along towards the downstairs window, his back against the panelled wood of the fence. He held his breath as the lock of the back door turned. This was not how it was supposed to happen. This wasn't the film he'd imagined.

— Ryan. *Psssssst.* Are you there?

Eve's voice let all the tension out of his body. He stepped along the fence and saw her leaning out of the back door in a white vest. The silver light on her bare shoulders.

— I'm here.

Eve smiled and brought her finger to her lips.

— Shh. Hold on.

She ducked back inside and the kitchen light clicked off.

Ryan stepped on to the patio and stood in front of the step to the back door. Eve stood in the open doorway in her vest and jogging bottoms. Her hair was tied back in a high ponytail. She smiled again.

— I knew you'd come.

Ryan felt the muscles in his cheeks as he smiled back at her.

— I wasn't happy with that goodbye.

His fingers squeezed the tape in his hand. Eve pulled the door nearly closed behind her and stood on the step. Her bare feet were pale against the concrete.

— Me either.

Ryan held up the tape.

— I made you this.

He watched her look at the dark cassette.

— I couldn't find a case, sorry.

Eve smiled.

— What is it?

— Some stuff I wanted to say. Just to you.

He held it out towards her. Eve stared at him as her hand took the tape.

— I won't let anyone hear.

Ryan shook his head.

— It's been a crazy night.

— Yeah?

Ryan heard the voice from his boom box in his head and smiled again.

— Let's just say I believe in the universe stuff.

Eve stepped forward to the edge of the step, her chin level with his eyes.

— You're kinda small for a boy.

Ryan lifted his chin and smiled.

— I'm still growing.

He reached out a hand and placed it on her hip, his eyes never leaving hers.

— You know if this was a film, this is where we'd kiss.

Eve tilted her head.

— Really?

— Yeah, the strings would start to build and the camera would start moving around us and going up and everybody in the cinema would breathe in and the strings would get louder and the credits would—

She held his face in her hands as she kissed him.

Ryan closed his eyes and felt everything he wanted to say travel through his lips into hers and, as his fingertips felt the line where the edge of her vest met her skin, he got the feeling that somehow this was just the beginning.

ACKNOWLEDGMENTS

Thank you Yael for helping me get to the heart of any half-decent idea I've ever had.

Mum and Naomi for your constant support. Sol and Dylan for unlimited ideas and inspiration. Nick for your trust and subtlety. Tom, Lily, Sam, Hannah and the whole HarperCollins team for your excitement and guidance (chuffed to be with you). Thank you Laura, for introducing me to Cathryn. Cathryn for thinking I had potential and speaking like a real person. Kim for waking me up from a five-year sleep and showing me it's OK to like both Steven Seagal and Toni Morrison. Thank you Miss Piggot, for starting 'story week' in third year infants and lighting a fire in my gut.

In a world already crammed full of so much stuff, thank you for reading my story.

Steven

IT'S ABOUT
LOVE

STEVEN CAMDEN

He's Luke. She's Leia.

Just like in *Star Wars*.
Just like they're
made for each other.
Same film studies course,
different backgrounds,
different ends of town.

Only this isn't a film.
This is real life.
This is where monsters
from the past come back
to take revenge.

This is where *you* are
sometimes the monster.
And where the things
we build to protect us,
can end up doing
the most harm…

04.06.15

Black.

The hum of a strip light. Radio static
as a dial tries to find a station.

Fade up to a face.

Young man. Wheat-coloured skin. Dark
hair cropped close.

The radio static settles on something old
- muffled Sinatra.

Emergency Room.

Molded red plastic chairs and cream
walls.

Young man stares out, thick shoulders
slumped.

Dark butterfly of blood spread across
the chest of his white shirt.

A Policewoman sits in chair to his right,
her body turned towards him.

POLICEWOMAN: Do you understand me?

Young man just stares out.

Sinatra's crackled chorus.
Circular clock on wall above them says
II.30pm.

POLICEWOMAN: I need you to tell me what
happened.

Young man frowns.
Cut to black.

YOUNG MAN (VOICEOVER): Start where it
matters, he said. Start in a moment where
things hang in the balance. Start with a
question. Then you can go back to wherever
you like. That's fine, but you show me one
moment where things don't hang in the
balance. Go on. Exactly. So where to start?

PART I.
Waiting.

Diagonal rain.

I'm standing under the bus shelter outside the crappy little shopping arcade. I'm wearing my battered blue hand-me-down Carhartt jacket, but I'm gonna get soaked walking up the hill.

It's Friday morning, last day of my first week.

Wait for the rain to stop and be late, or walk into the room like a drowned rat? Either way, I'm gonna get stared at.

It's been a week of sitting in circles wearing sticky labels with our names on. Most of them seem to already know each other from schools around here. Kids who look like money. Who speak with words my brain uses, but my mouth runs a mile from. Kids not like me.

"No umbrella?"

She's wearing one of those long black Northface coats that cost like a hundred and fifty quid. The top half of her face is hidden by the massive umbrella she's holding on her shoulder, but I can see her mouth and her chin and chunky plaits of dark hair either side of her neck. I look over my shoulder, then back at her, "You talking to me?"

She tilts her umbrella back and I see her face. She's mixed race. Nice eyes. Tiny freckles dot her cheeks. She's smiling. *No, she's staring.* "Yeah, Travis, I'm talking to you."

Rain trickles off the edges of her umbrella, her safe underneath.

I feel to look away. She frowns,

"Travis Bickle? *Taxi Driver?*"

I know who she means, but I don't move.

She holds her left hand out in front of her like a gun, pointing at me. I watch the rain hit her fingers and notice a ring that looks like a mini snowdome made of amber, "Well I'm the only one here."

Her voice is scratchy but well-spoken. *She's staring.* I look down. Tight jeans and black All Stars stick out from the bottom of her coat.

"You're doing film studies, right?" she says.

I look up, turning my head slightly, trying not to seem uncomfortable. *She's staring.*

Her eyebrows are raised, "I saw you in the circle the other day," she says. My stomach and shoulders tighten.

She points at her umbrella. "You wanna share?"

I stare past her at the entrance to the arcade and feel her eyes on me as I shake my head, "Nah, I'm good."

She shrugs, "OK. See you up there, Travis."

And she walks away.

I watch her umbrella float through the rain to the traffic lights, cross the road, then turn into the church graveyard and out of sight.

Good choice.

I stare at my phone. 8:50am, Friday, 6th September. Seven sleeps left.

What's he doing right now?

An old woman walks under the shelter to my right, pumping her little purple umbrella like a Super Soaker. She looks at me, "It's not dry is it?"

She opens her bag and starts looking for something. I watch the rain fall off the edge of the shelter roof. "I said, it's not dry is it young man?"

I turn to her. She stares at my face. Her hair is the colour of cobwebs. *What you looking at?*

"Strong silent type are we?"

I don't answer as I walk out into the rain.

I chose to come here.

I chose to catch two buses to reach a college on the other side of town.

They had film studies at the Community College, which I could've walked to. Tommy started as a builder's apprentice for his uncle, and Zia had to take the supermarket job, to prove to his dad he's dedicated enough to join the family business, so it's not like I would've been with them anyway. But I still chose to come here.

A place far enough away that nobody knows me. A place where nobody's heard his name.

I walk in the classroom soaked.

Everyone stares.

I try to tilt my face down without making it obvious. *Get your head up you idiot.* The tables are arranged in a squared horseshoe facing the front. No more circles and name badges. The teacher guy's half sitting, half leaning on his desk. I look straight to the back of the room. The umbrella girl's sitting in the back left hand corner. The chair next to her is empty.

"Is it raining?" says Teacher Guy.

A few people laugh. I feel my face getting hot as I scan the room for another empty seat. There aren't any. "Have a seat," says the teacher, "we're just talking favourite films". His voice is local, with a bit of somewhere else mixed in. He's younger than most teachers I've known, but what does that really mean?

I avoid everyone's eyes as I walk to the back and sit down next to Umbrella Girl. The ring on her finger has something inside the amber, and I think of the mosquito from *Jurassic Park*. She doesn't look at me. *Don't look at her then.*

Teacher Guy ca rries on,

"So. We've had *Twilight*, *Avatar*, and, what was the last one?"

A kid with blonde hair and a suntan puts his hand up, "Avengers sir."

The teacher guy points at him, "Right. *The Avengers*. Thank you. You can put your hand down, and less of the sir, OK? I'm Noah. We'll stick to first names I think."

Great. Another 'cool' teacher who wants to be friends. 'Call me Noah, I'm just like you, let's be mates'. Tell you what, Noah, let's not, yeah? Hows about you just teach us a bunch of stuff about film and shove the rest of it up—

"Is there anyone here whose favourite film isn't a huge Hollywood blockbuster? Not that there's anything wrong with blockbusters, but something different. How about you, at the back, Water Boy?"

He means me. More people laugh. The blonde kid's staring back. I spotted him the first day. He looks like he should be in a toothpaste advert. Hot needles prick my face as my hands ball into fists under the table.

Teacher Guy's standing up now and I can tell he takes care of himself. His hair's the dark curly bush mine would be if I let it grow, but he's got that stubble I'm years away from having. Through his light-blue linen shirt his shoulders look strong. Noah.

I dunno if I could take him, but he'd know he'd been in a fight.

He's staring at me. Everyone is. Umbrella Girl's turned in her seat. *Better choose something good.* I can taste rain as I stare forward and say, "*Leon.*"

Noah's face flickers briefly and his stare changes, like he's gone from just waiting for my answer to trying to see behind my face. Other people in the room look confused as their eyes go from me, to him, then back to me again and, even though I don't want to be looked at, I feel good. I've surprised him. The blonde kid's staring back at Umbrella Girl and I can feel her smiling on my right. Noah's still staring at me, his head tilted like he's remembering something. Then he nods, "I see. Interesting choice."

Umbrella Girl sticks her hand up.

"I love that film too, sir, I mean, Noah."

Noah looks at her, then at me and it's kind of like everyone else goes out of focus.

"Alright then. You two can be partners."

He claps his hands and everyone's back.

"Right. Everybody turn to the person next to you. If you don't know them, introduce yourself and you've got fifteen minutes. I want discussions; best films, worst films, important films, funniest films, films that matter. Get everything down, make notes, scribbles, doesn't matter, no idea is stupid, get talking. Go!"

Shuffling and chatter. The blonde kid's looking back. I wipe my forehead with the back of my hand

and cold water runs down to my elbow.

"It's a love story you know. *Leon*."

She's doodling on the cover of a new A4 lined pad. I stare at her amber ring as I peel off my jacket and let it hang inside out over the chair. My black T-shirt is dry, but my arms are cold as I take my notebook out of my bag. It's a new one. Ring-bound. I pull my Biro out from the binding and take the top off, purposely tensing my bicep more than I need to. I'm glad she's on my right.

I don't look at her, "No it's not."

I start to write the date, like we're still in school, then scribble it out hoping she didn't notice.

"Course it is," she says, "Not a conventional one, but it's a story about love."

The fact that she's even seen *Leon* makes me like her, but it's not a love story.

"It's about revenge," I say.

My right arm is still tensed as I scribble over the date again and I can smell cucumber shampoo. Umbrella Girl stops doodling,

"No, revenge is what starts it, what she thinks she wants, but it's about sacrifice. The choice to love."

Her skin's the colour of wet sand, like Dad's, and her ear has almost no lobe at the bottom, like an elf.

"I guess we saw it differently," I say.

"Which is why it's so good! Tragic love story. Amazing soundtrack, too. I'm Leia."

I blink longer than I should do. *You're kidding me.*

She drops her pen and holds out her hand, her amber ring is almost glowing. *Leia?* I look around the class. Everyone's deep in discussion and right now, in the moment, I feel older.

I shake her hand. It's half the width of mine.

"It's not my only favourite film, yeah? I like other stuff too. I'm Luke."

Leia smiles, "Course you are."

Whenever I go to a new place I always imagine it as a movie set. I think about how every brick and wall and door and corner and roof had to be chosen and built by somebody. How the people who move through and around the spaces are characters playing their roles and, most of all, I'm aware that at all times, somebody could be watching.

Nobody knows me here. I'm that stranger without a past. An empty page of a person that I can fill with whatever I want and that's all they'll have to go on. I can be in control for once. My choices. My story.
But the voice I hear says different. The voice I can't hide from is telling me that it doesn't matter where I go. What I do, or tell people.

None of it matters, because in a week he'll be home and anything that's happened since he's been gone will get blown out of the water.

Maybe this is what will save me when he gets home. Coming here. Meeting Leia. I can't change the past, but maybe I can hide from it. Maybe I can be someone else...

TAPE

KEEP IN THE LOOP WITH
STEVEN CAMDEN

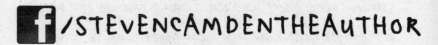 /STEVENCAMDENTHEAUTHOR